TWO SCREENPLAYS

JAMES HOWERTON

iUniverse, Inc.
Bloomington

TWO SCREENPLAYS

iUniverse books may be ordered through booksellers or by contacting:

iUniverse
1663 Liberty Drive
Bloomington, IN 47403
www.iuniverse.com
1-800-Authors (1-800-288-4677)

ISBN: 978-1-4759-3833-3 (sc)
ISBN: 978-1-4759-3834-0 (ebk)

Printed in the United States of America

iUniverse rev. date: 07/09/2012

THE RED CHICK

Lincoln, Nebraska
March 1950

(A building on the corner of 48th and Cotner Boulevard. Bryan Hospital, the sign reads. It is a cold, windy day. A 1948 Packard drives into the hospital and parks. Three women get out: Molly Kendrick, age 81, a frail woman who walks with a cane; her daughter Betsy, 62 and her grand-daughter Amy, age 32. Their dress and jewelry indicate substantial wealth)

BETSY

Don't go tramping off, Mom. Wait for us.

MOLLY

I want to get this over with. I've wasted enough of my life in the doctor's office.

AMY

Here, Grandma, let me walk with you.

(Amy takes her grandmother's arm and the three women walk slowly up the concrete stairs out of the wind and into the hospital)

[Fade to] . . .

(Betsy and Amy are sitting in a waiting room. Finally Molly bustles in, adjusting her dress with a series of irritated grunts. She leans her cane and sits down in the waiting room and immediately takes a bolt of cotton thread out of her purse, and knitting needles. She begins to knit, humming softly)

BETSY

(Watching her)

Mom, what did Dr. Tracey say?

MOLLY

He said to wait here. He wants to talk to all of us.

(A long silence)

AMY

About what, Grandma?

(Molly pauses in her knitting, frowns down at her hands).

MOLLY

These old claws can't even knit anymore.

AMY

Grandma—about what?

MOLLY

I don't know, Honey. I only know that it probably won't be a pleasure to hear.

BETSY

Maybe it's just the flu, like before.

MOLLY

No, he'd have told me that when he was back there poking and prodding. He knew what it was before I ever came in here today, but he wanted to be sure. Doctors make a lot more money being sure than not.

AMY

Grandma, don't talk like that.

BETSY

(Her voice lightly trembling)

It could be something minor, Mom.

MOLLY

Damn—I can hardly knit anymore. And my hands were always so sure.

(Finally Dr. Tracey enters the waiting room. He has a gentle and sad look on his face that does not bode well)

MOLLY

Well, let's hear it, Marvin.

(Dr. Tracey glances at Betsy, then Amy. He gives Molly a half-smile)

DR. TRACEY

You always did like to get straight to the point, Molly.

MOLLY

(Watching him cautiously)

It's cancer, isn't it?

DR. TRACEY

Yes, Molly, it's cancer. It's in your liver and your kidneys.

(A shocked silence. Then Betsy and Amy burst into tears)

BETSEY

Oh God, Mom! Oh no!

AMY

Grandma!

MOLLY

I suspected it was in the kidneys, anyway. The last few times I peed it felt unnatural down there.

(Looks at Dr. Tracey)

It can't be treated, of course.

DR. TRACEY

No, Molly. I'm sorry.

BETSY

Oh God, Mom!

MOLLY

Well, then you know the last question, Marvin.

DR. TRACEY

(Studies her for a moment)

Two months, Molly. Maybe three.

[Scene fades with Dr. Tracey's voice]: "I'm going to prescribe morphine pills, Molly, and . . ."

(Betsy and Molly get into the car. Amy slips into the back seat. She is weeping)

BETSY

(Bursts into sobs)

Oh, Mom! Oh God, Mom!

MOLLY

Here, Baby.

(Molly holds her daughter, strokes her hair, lets her sob on an old bony shoulder)

Oh, Betsy. It's going to be all right.

<u>BETSY</u>

Mom . . . I'm scared, Mom!

<u>MOLLY</u>

No, no. Don't cry. It comes to all of us.

<u>AMY</u>

(Crying)

Grandma . . . what's going to happen?

<u>MOLLY</u>

I don't know, Honey. And I don't care. I only know that it's about time.

[Cut to] . . .

(Molly's house, a large and spacious colonial mansion near the downtown Lincoln area. She is directing her grandson, Willie, to load about twelve diary books into her 1948 Packard. Willie is 26, a handsome and doting grandson)

<u>WILLIE</u>

Why am I loading books into your car, Grandma?

<u>MOLLY</u>

Put them right there on the passenger seat, Willie. My God, when a woman gets so old that she can't carry a pile of books—that should be the end. All right, now there's another load of them in the garage. I'm going to give them to Mr. Harrison there at the plant. His eldest daughter has an interest in becoming a writer. Thank you, Willie.

<u>WILLIE</u>

Grandma . . . what are you doing?

<u>MOLLY</u>

(Gives him an arch look)

I'm going on a visit. That's what they used to call it long ago, a visit. They didn't say trip or vacation, they called it a visit.

WILLIE

I'll drive you then.

MOLLY

No. This is a visit I have to take alone.

WILLIE

Grandma . . . you're not going to try and drive . . .

MOLLY

It's my car. I can drive it if I please.

WILLIE

Grandma, no you can't. It would be breaking the law—they took your license away ten years ago.

MOLLY

I remember. I'm not senile yet.

WILLIE

Please, Grandma. I can drive you wherever you need to go. I'm going to have to tell Mom if you try and—

MOLLY

Don't you dare! Remember the time I snuck you into Missouri to buy fire-crackers and bring them back Illegally into Nebraska? And when you smashed your dad's car and I committed perjury and told him it was me? I'm cashing those chips in, Willie. Don't you dare rat on me, to your mother or the cops. This is my car, and I'll damn well drive it if I please.

WILLIE

Grandma, just let me drive you there; I can take you where you need to go, and—

MOLLY

(Cuts him off with a wave of her hand. Smiles)

6

No, my darling grandson—you can't. Now please get those books.

[Cut to] . . .

(The Packard lurches down a gravel road and comes to a huge poultry plant. Trucks are grinding into the place. A large sign: KENDRICK POULTRY.

Molly pulls the car into the complex, nearly smashing a gatepost. Lincoln Harrison, a black man of fifty, an employee of Kendrick, the groundskeeper, is spraying weeds that have crept out of the concrete pavement of the parking lot. He smiles at the Packard, then wanders over)

LINCOLN

Mrs. Kendrick! How nice to see you.

MOLLY

Mr. Harrison, I'm glad to see you too.

LINCOLN

What brings you out for a visit on such a fine day?

MOLLY

Well, for one I brought you a pile of books. They're back there. I think Sylvia might enjoy a few of them.

LINCOLN

Oh, my God, books. And I'll try to enjoy a few of them myself.

(Lincoln opens the back door and takes out a bulging sack)

I can't thank you enough, Mrs. Kendrick.

(Studies her)

And why else did you come to visit, if I might ask?

MOLLY

(Looks over at him)

I just wanted to see the old farm again. I'll drive down there under that burr oak tree. And I'll just sit awhile; then I'll be gone.

LINCOLN

(Studies her with a fond, sad smile)

You know you're free to go anywhere in this plant you want to go, Mrs. Kendrick.

MOLLY

No, I'll just park this thing under that burr oak tree. I'll sit awhile; then I'll be gone.

LINCOLN

That tree's a burr oak, is it? I always wondered what it was.

MOLLY

Someone once said that the burr oak is a forever tree.

LINCOLN

How's that, Mrs. Kendrick?

MOLLY

Oh, a tree that goes on after . . . a tree that goes on, that's all.

LINCOLN

(smiles)

Well, Mrs. Kendrick, I been looking at that tree for thirty years now. I hate to say it, but it's not what I'd call an attractive tree.

MOLLY

(She laughs)

No, it isn't. I've said that many times myself.

LINCOLN

(Glances into the car at the diaries)

You going to do some reading, Mrs. Kendrick?

MOLLY

Yes, a little reading, under that tree. Then I'll be gone.

(Molly lurches the Packard across an expanse of grass and the car cries to a stop just in time to keep from slamming into the burr oak tree. Molly shuts off the car. There is only the soft wind. A sunny, cloud-smeared day.

Molly stares at the great complex, the factory, the endless modern hatcheries gone far beyond the eye. The wind blows softly. She stares at a crumbled red stump sticking out of the ground, an ancient well pump that they hadn't bothered to get rid of.

As she stares at the great poultry plant, it begins to melt away to) . . .

(A crumbling shack on a windblown and scrubby farm ten miles south of the new city of Lincoln, Nebraska.

It is early June, in the year 1885. Down the dirt road a rider appears. He has a packhorse behind him, carrying a load of supplies.

Molly has just turned 16, and she and her best friend Lois are hiding behind a hillock, watching the rider)

MOLLY

He's back because his dad died.

LOIS

It looks like he's planning to stay awhile. Ha ha! Molly!

(Lois pinches Molly on the leg)

MOLLY

Ow! Lois, stop that. He went off and made some money in the east, and now he's looking this farm over to see what he can get out of it. Then he'll be gone. Mrs. Whithers in town told me all about it.

LOIS

If he's smart he will. And don't play dumb with me. I remember the sweet you had on him.

9

MOLLY

I was 12 years old when he took off. Now he's a twenty and three year old man.

LOIS

He left cuz of Louise Powers, you know.

MOLLY

I know. Get down, Lois! He'll see us.

(Thomas Kendrick rides up to the abandoned shack. He gets wearily off his horse and surveys the place, the house and weathered buildings, the scrub prairie. He glances at the hill over the farm and spies the two girls watching him. He smiles and tips his hat)

LOIS

He saw us, Molly.

MOLLY

I know. But if he really is back to stay, we should make him welcome. That's what the Bible says.

LOIS

Ha. Molly, don't even think of it. Thomas Kendrick? He's 23 years old.

MOLLY

Think of what?

LOIS

You know what.

[Cut to] . . .

(Thomas Kendrick is replacing cedar shingles on the roof of the farmhouse. It is a mild, sunny day, early summer. He pulls out rotted shingles and tosses them to the ground, then fits new shingles in and hammers them down. He takes a break, wiping the sweat from his forehead. He stares to the north, where a figure is walking across the windblown pasture.

Molly approaches. Thomas is squatting on the farmhouse roof. At first he watches her as if she were a ghost; then he scrambles to put on a shirt)

THOMAS

Ma'am?

MOLLY

I—I brought you a—well, it's kind of a welcome home present.

THOMAS

(Smiles down at her, a skinny little barefoot farm-girl in a worn grey dress, scared as a rabbit)

A welcome present. It looks like a pie.

MOLLY

(Embarrassed)

Well, it is. Yes, it's a pie. It's Blackcherry.

THOMAS

That sounds good. I guess I'll have to climb down and have a piece.

MOLLY

(Staring at the ground)

Oh you don't have to stop your work or any of that. I just thought you might like a pie. It's Blackcherry. They were fruiting like crazy down at the creek last year, and we put them up like crazy.

THOMAS

My favorite. Let's have some pie.

(Thomas climbs down and they go into the farmhouse. Thomas has improved it considerably; but it is still a raw work in progress. Molly gulps at her throat as she enters)

THOMAS

Here, have a seat. If I share pie with you, I should know your name.

MOLLY

(Smiles)

You don't remember me, do you?

THOMAS

(Stares at her a moment. His eyes grow wide)

Molly! Little Molly Simmons. My God. I'm sorry, I should have known you on the spot.

MOLLY

(turning red)

That's all right. You been gone four years.

THOMAS

You turned into a beautiful young lady.

MOLLY

(Turning bright red)

Well, I'm sixteen now.

THOMAS

(Playing the host)

What would you like to drink with your pie, Molly? I have water, and I have water. And I'm afraid it's water from the creek.

MOLLY

(Smiling)

I don't mind creek water. I've had it before. It's gritty, but it's wet.

THOMAS

I'll bet you made this pie yourself.

MOLLY

Yes. It ain't—isn't nothing making a Blackcherry pie from preserves. I just thought you might like a . . .

THOMAS

(Smiles at her)

Welcome home gift.

MOLLY

Yeah, that.

(She stares away, embarrassed)

It looks like from all your work you might be planning to stay here.

THOMAS

Well, I hope to. The old man, bless his soul, left me this land and this house—such as it is. I've got something that I can maybe make something of. Oh, this is good pie. The best I've tasted since—ever.

MOLLY

(Grinning, embarrassed)

We don't have no sugar, so I used honey on the top of it. My Dad says it's crazy trying to start a farm here in Nebraska.

THOMAS

(Looks at her in surprise)

Do I look crazy?

(Thomas makes a comical crazy-face)

13

MOLLY

(Giggles as she eats her pie)

No. I hope you stay. What I mean is; it'd be nice if you stayed.

THOMAS

(Smiling)

Why, Molly?

MOLLY

I don't know!

[Fade to] . . .

(The farmyard. Molly has come across the pasture from her place to visit with Thomas. He takes a break, resting his weary back against a porch post)

MOLLY

You been working pretty hard out here. After I'm done with my chores, I could come over here and help you out—or what. I'm as good and hard a worker as any.

THOMAS

Don't you have school?

MOLLY

No, I never went to school. Dad said it was a waste of good work time. Especially for a girl.

THOMAS

(Smiling)

So what kind of work can you do, Molly?

MOLLY

I can hammer nails, paint wood. I'm a good cook, too.

(She blooms red, suddenly embarrassed)

THOMAS

All right. I could use some help, and some company. So long as your mom and dad don't mind. I'll hire you at twenty-five cents a day. How's that?

MOLLY

You don't have to pay me money. I'd like to help you fix the place up.

THOMAS

No. If you work for me, you'll get paid. And I'm going to see to it that you work.

MOLLY

A quarter a day, I'll work like you never saw.

THOMAS

I'm sure you know how to put in a garden.

MOLLY

I can put in a garden better than anybody.

(She looks at the scrubby weed patch south of the house, what was once a garden plot)

It's late in the season. Maybe too late for potatoes. We'd have to plant quick crops that you can store for the winter.

THOMAS

You'll have to carry water up from the creek.

MOLLY

Oh, it's only a hundred yards or so.

THOMAS

I do have a couple of new pumps coming from Omaha; one for the house well and another for the outside well.

15

MOLLY

(Studying the garden plot)

String beans. They grow fast. Squash and carrots—maybe even try a few potatoes.

THOMAS

All right, you're in charge of the garden. Twenty-five cents a day.

[Fades to] . . .

(A series of scenes as summer progresses: Molly hoeing the garden, Thomas repairing fence. Molly lugging water from the creek, Thomas installing the outside pump. They stand together and admire the pump that stands gleaming red in the sun. Molly and Thomas shooing calves into the pasture, Thomas repairing the chicken house) . . .

[Fade to] . . .

(A hot day in late July. Molly pours water from a bucket onto a hill of sprawling yellow-and-green squash plants. She pauses to wipe the sweat from her face. Then she spies a horse-drawn carriage approaching from the main road.

Thomas is out repairing the gate. He sees the carriage approach, and takes off his hat. Molly squats down to pull weeds from the garden. She glances at the fine covered-and-fringed carriage pulled by two purebred Arabian horses.

Louise Powers drives the carriage into the yard. Thomas watches her, his eyes stunned. Louise gives him a sad smile. Her face is droopy, and it's apparent that she's been drinking)

LOUISE

Thomas. It's been a long time.

THOMAS

Four years—that's not long.

LOUISE

It seems so. When I heard you had come back, I thought it was to sell this place and be gone.

THOMAS

A lot of folks seemed to think that.

LOUISE

Yes . . . well.

(She stares down at Molly, barefoot in the dirt, pulling weeds. Louise's drunken eyes try to focus. Thomas stands uncomfortable, looking away at the prairie)

THOMAS

Well, it's good to see you again—Louise.

LOUISE

Is it?

(She smiles down at Molly)

That's the little Simmons girl. She must be—what, sixteen by now?

THOMAS

Sixteen and a half. I've hired her to put in a garden.

LOUISE

Hired her, have you? I'll drink to that.

(She startles him by removing a silver flask from her dress and taking a swig. Molly stares up wide-eyed from the garden)

Care for a drink, Thomas? I had to drink to get up the courage to come here, you see.

THOMAS

No, thank you.

LOUISE

(Looks down at Molly)

Hello, little girl.

THOMAS

Louise, I don't know if this is a good time—

LOUISE

Oh, I'll behave. I promise.

THOMAS

Where's Mason?

LOUISE

Do you mean Mason, my beloved husband? He's passed out by now, I'm sure.

THOMAS

Passed out—drunk?

LOUISE

He does much of his drinking late into the night—he says it helps him concentrate on business. It also aids him in avoiding the marriage bed.

(Molly stares up blinking her eyes)

THOMAS

Yes. Well, Louise, it's good to see you and all. You probably should—

LOUISE

Aren't you going to invite me into your house for some refreshment?

THOMAS

I don't have a lot in the way of refreshment.

LOUISE

That's all right, I've brought my own. I want to invite you to a party I'm planning, and I want to see what you've done to this place.

(Molly watches them enter the farmhouse with worried eyes. She continues to pull weeds, but lifts her head when she hears loud accusations, tense voices. Louise Powers suddenly bursts out of the house and stumbles to her fine carriage. She manages to climb into the vehicle; then slaps the purebred horses into a trot. Molly, wide-eyed, watches her dust trail)

LOUISE

(Yells behind her):

You're invited too, little girl!

(Thomas comes out of the house, scratching his head. He stares at the carriage disappearing into the green hills. He looks at Molly, puzzled and slightly embarrassed)

THOMAS

That was Louise Powers.

MOLLY

I know who she is.

THOMAS

Came over for some kind of visit, I guess. I don't know why she came over, but it's strange.

MOLLY

Why's it strange?

THOMAS

(Looks at Molly)

I don't know. It's been four years. I was engaged to be married to her.

MOLLY

What happened?

THOMAS

What happened? Oh, I didn't have any money. Dad and I were just surviving on this place. I thought if I could go back east I could make some money, save it up and come back with a good enough stake to make a go of it.

MOLLY

Well, didn't you?

THOMAS

(Stares away)

I suppose.

MOLLY

And didn't she want to wait for you?

THOMAS

No, she didn't.

MOLLY

Why?

THOMAS

Oh, she fell in love with another guy. A guy with money.

MOLLY

Mr. Powers.

THOMAS

You're kind of a nosey little thing, aren't you?

MOLLY

No—well, I don't mean to be.

THOMAS

(Staring down the road)

That was a hell of a strange thing.

(Looks at Molly)

She invited me to a party, believe it or not. That was before she began yelling and crying.

MOLLY

A party? She's drunk, though, isn't she?

THOMAS

Yes, she's very drunk. A party at the Powers "manor", three weeks from now. I don't know why she'd show up out of the blue and invite me to something like that.

MOLLY

Don't you know?

THOMAS

(Glances at her)

I know you're an eavesdropper. And your mother tells me you're a good seamstress. You could probably make a dress in three weeks.

MOLLY

What?

THOMAS

The party is three weeks from now. Her husband's birthday. I'm sure she invited me to give poor Mason a jab of the knife—but free food and dancing shouldn't be passed up. She probably won't remember it, but she invited you—I heard her.

MOLLY

What do you mean, dress?

THOMAS

I'm asking you to attend the party with me, Molly. It might be fun. Food and dancing and fun. You work too much, and so do I. We could both use a break.

MOLLY

(Staring at him)

You're asking me to go to a party with you? To the Powers mansion. Dad wouldn't let me do that, mix with rich people and have them make fun of me.

THOMAS

Why would they make fun of you?

MOLLY

I don't know! I wouldn't know how to act. But I can make a dress . . .

THOMAS

Well, talk to your Mom about it, and have her talk to your Dad. That is, if you want to go with me.

MOLLY

You want to take me to a party.

THOMAS

Yes. And if you decide not to attend, then I won't attend. You either attend the party with me, or I sit home alone.

MOLLY

I'd be scared going to something like that. I don't have shoes. I don't know how to dance or anything.

THOMAS

I wish I could teach you, but I can't dance either, not without looking the fool. We can eat. There should be lots of rich food there. I'll buy you shoes, on credit.

MOLLY

You want to take me to a party . . .

[Fade to] . . .

(Thomas drives his wagon into the Simmons place. It is a scrub-poor farm. The house is a grey, shabby thing surrounded by windblown shacks where a cow moos and chickens squawk and pigs grunt in the mud. Earl Simmons, Molly's father, crab-walks out of the house. He is a scrawny, mean-faced man who all his life complained of a bad back. He squints at Thomas, who climbs down from the wagon)

EARL

She's not but sixteen, you know.

THOMAS

I know, Sir. But she works harder than two men, and she deserves a night of fun.

EARL

What do you mean by fun?

THOMAS

Sir, don't question my intentions—or my integrity.

(The farmhouse door squeals open and Maude Simmons escorts her daughter Molly down the porch steps. Molly wears a sky-blue dress and her auburn hair is done up with pins. Thomas smiles)

You look beautiful, Molly.

MOLLY

Thank you.

EARL

You get her home no later than twelve midnight. We have a clock in there that tells perfect time.

MAUDE

Oh Dad, let her go.

[Fade to] . . .

(The Powers mansion, a white colonial wedding cake of a house, on a hill so tall that the city of Lincoln can be seen in the distance. Molly and Thomas get down from the wagon and enter the place, arm in arm. Neighbors, ranchers and farmers welcome them. The mansion is lit by a hundred kerosene lamps and a thousand scented candles. Molly stares around her, amazed)

MOLLY

This is scary. Everybody's looking at me.

23

THOMAS

They're looking at you because you're the prettiest girl in the room.

MOLLY

What are you supposed to do, now that you're at the party?

THOMAS

You eat, you drink, you enjoy yourself. You dance.

MOLLY

No, I couldn't ever do that. Dad told me not to do anything that'd make them laugh at me.

(Mason Powers approaches them. He nods to Thomas. Thomas nods back. Mason is happily drunk)

MASON

Welcome to my home, Thomas. Please enjoy yourselves. This is Miss Simmons?

THOMAS

Yes. Molly Simmons.

MASON

(Amused)

Miss Simmons, our home is yours. I hope you enjoy yourself, and I hope you will forgive my wife. She has taken too much tonic this night, and is her usual charming self.

[Fade to] . . .

(Molly is standing munching on a treat from the food table, a deviled egg. She looks up at Louise Powers, who approaches her, stumbling drunk, wearing a cold smile. Music plays, and in the background folks are dancing. Molly wipes the deviled egg from her lips)

LOUISE

Hello, little girl.

MOLLY

Hello. This is a wonderful party, Mrs. Powers.

LOUISE

I'm glad you came. Your dress is plain and homespun, but that, of course, only makes it prettier.

MOLLY

Ma'am?

LOUISE

Yes, I'm drunk, little girl. You're very pretty. But Thomas needs more than pretty.

MOLLY

What?

LOUISE

Thomas is—he is a man who needs intellectual stimulation. He loves to work, to build things—but he's deeper than you know.

MOLLY

Why are you saying this to me?

LOUISE

Because I see how he looks at you. Because I see in you what I lost. Thomas sees a young, innocent prairie girl like you, with windblown hair and a pretty face. But when the bloom wears off, he is going to want conversation.

MOLLY

I'm sorry. I don't know what you're talking about.

LOUISE

Conversation. That is what love is. Do you read and write—Molly?

MOLLY

(Gives her a look)

I'm sorry, Mrs. Powers; and I thank you for inviting me here—but I don't think that's your business.

LOUISE

(Smiles)

I don't mean to be cruel, little girl. Tonight, on the eve of my husband's fortieth birthday, I'm awash in regrets. Of course you're in love with Thomas.

MOLLY

Mrs. Powers, I don't know what you're talking about.

LOUISE

I'm no fool, and neither are you.

[Cut to] . . .

(Thomas and Molly trying to dance. They trip over themselves as the small orchestra from Lincoln plays a waltz)

MOLLY

Oh God! I'm stumbling like a calf.

THOMAS

Smile and have fun, Molly. When you're dancing the worst thing you can think about is how you look.

MOLLY

(Catching Thomas as he lurches comically)

You're doing worse than me.

THOMAS

I am!

MOLLY

And you're doing it on purpose.

[Fade to] . . .

(Thomas and Molly are standing in the manicured garden of the Powers estate. Lincoln glows faintly across the dark prairie. The small orchestra plays a sad tune. The cello sings mournfully across the prairie)

THOMAS

It's going on eleven, Molly. I'd better get you home. Did you have a good time?

MOLLY

I did. Except that with Mrs. Powers. She doesn't like me.

THOMAS

Don't worry about it.

[Cut to] . . .

(They ride to the Simmons place in the wagon. The wind is blowing sweet across the prairie)

THOMAS

I hope you had fun, Molly.

MOLLY

It was the best night I ever had.

THOMAS

Good. It was the best night I ever had too.

MOLLY

No . . . it was?

THOMAS

Yes, it was.

(Thomas drives the wagon into the Simmons yard. He jumps out and helps Molly down. She laughs nervously)

THOMAS

Thank you, Miss Simmons, for a wonderful evening. I hope you enjoyed it.

MOLLY

It was the best night of my life.

THOMAS

Then, I think I should ask you for a good-night kiss.

MOLLY

(Turns scarlet)

A kiss? Oh God . . .

(They kiss. The wind blows across the prairie, which suddenly melts into the industrial plant—1950—the trucks, the rusted pump. The corporate complex that now sends eggs and poultry far across the nation. The modern age suddenly stands in the wind, in front of her.

Molly, 81 years old, stares away, remembering that first kiss) . . .

[Cut to] . . .

(Lincoln Harrison is spraying weeds outside the office building, when the door swings open and Jud Edwards steps out. He stares at the Packard under the burr oak tree. He approaches Lincoln Harrison)

EDWARDS

Linck—what the hell. That's Mrs. Kendrick's car, isn't it?

HARRISON

That it is.

EDWARDS

Betsy called me a while ago and wanted to know if she was here, and I told her no, Mrs. Kendrick wasn't here.

HARRISON

Why'd you tell her that?

EDWARDS

I thought it was true! I didn't know old Mrs. Kendrick was out here. What's she doing over there?

HARRISON

I think she's reading. And I'm sure she wants to be left alone.

EDWARDS

Reading? What?

HARRISON

(Staring at the Packard)

Diaries, I think. She gave me a whole sack-full of books.

EDWARDS

Old Mrs. Kendrick gave you books?

HARRISON

I think she gave them more to my daughter than to me.

EDWARDS

(Shakes his head at the Packard)

Are we all going to be getting presents from her?

HARRISON

I kind of doubt it.

EDWARDS

You heard about what the doctor said to her.

HARRISON

I heard.

EDWARDS

Well, I better get in there and phone Betsy . . . shouldn't I?

HARRISON

I don't think so. I think—I'm sure—that this particular day Mrs. Kendrick wouldn't want her reading disturbed.

EDWARDS

(Stares uncertainly at the Packard)

She in that bad a mood?

HARRISON

She wants to be left alone there. She of all people has earned that right—and she of all people is most likely to take your head off, if you tell on her. John, you don't know who's in that car. You can't see it from the office.

EDWARDS

She actually managed to drive here by herself?

HARRISON

That she did.

EDWARDS

I gotta call Betsy about this. What if the police are out looking for her?

HARRISON

I wouldn't do that, John. Not yet. She's just over there, sitting in her car. If you cause her to be interrupted, she might take your head off. I'll keep an eye on her.

EDWARDS

(Turns and marches away)

I didn't see nothing out here, Buddy! I'm doing inventory reports.

(Harrison makes a strange smile at the Packard, then goes on with his work)

[Fade to] . . .

(A cloudy day, early September. Thomas and Molly are cleaning out the root cellar behind the house, scraping and sweeping out dirt. Molly carries a cornstalk, which she uses to spin cobwebs out of the corners)

MOLLY

There've been rats down here.

THOMAS

I see. We'll have to mortar and seal her up. It's better than it looks; I'll have to work a little on the doors.

(A dog barks in the distance)

MOLLY

Oh God, that sounds like Bounce.

THOMAS

I wondered when your dog would follow you over here. Why the hell did you name him Bounce?

MOLLY

One time when he was a puppy I was out walking with him and he scared up a brace of grouse. When they flew out he got so excited he started bouncing up and down—(laughs as she demonstrates with her hands)—so I named him Bounce.

THOMAS

(Chuckling)

I'm glad he finally came to visit. I'm glad of today—I hope.

MOLLY

(Looks at him)

31

He's not supposed to be off the farm. That means the twins are coming.

(They climb out of the root cellar and Molly shades her eyes and gazes northward. Thomas strides over to the barn; then emerges with a raw hog bone. Bounce, a beagle-mutt, gallops up to Molly with a yelp, slobbering with excitement)

MOLLY

Bounce! What are you doing off the farm? You should be skinned.

(Thomas walks over. The dog stares at him warily)

THOMAS

Hello, Bounce. Here, I've got something for you. Luck for Bounce, I just butchered a hog. Here's a meat bone.

(Bounce edges up to him and snatches the bone from Thomas's hand. Bounce trots off and finds a place in the shade to chew)

MOLLY

That'll keep him busy for a while. Now he's going to be coming over here every day.

THOMAS

I could use the company.

(Stares north across the farm)

There they are.

(Twins, a boy and girl, eight years old, come running across the prairie. Stewart and Bonnie, Molly's brother and sister)

THOMAS

Ahhh! Indians! We're being attacked!

(The twins run up to Thomas, squealing and giggling)

Bonnie! Have you been a good girl?

BONNIE

(Giggling)

No!

THOMAS

Well, then—

(He grabs her up and lightly spanks her, making her burst out laughing)

And you, Chipmunk Stew; have you been a good boy?

STEW

No.

THOMAS

Argghh!

(Grabs up the laughing boy and gives him a spank)

You kids better go inside and make your sister fix you something to eat. Then you'd better get a candy.

(He passes Molly on his way back to the root cellar. She gives him a dark look)

MOLLY

I'm sorry. They're not supposed to be coming over here.

THOMAS

Well, I already promised them a meal.

(Thomas strides back to the root cellar and Molly marches up to the twins)

MOLLY

What are you two doing way over here? Dad'll skin you alive.

STEW

We was hungry.

MOLLY

Well, have Mom fix you some food. But you shouldn't go begging for it.

BONNIE

You know we can't do that.

STEW

And you got so much of it here. Mr. Kendrick said we could eat something.

BONNIE

He said we could have a candy too. And you got so much over here.

MOLLY

I don't have anything over here. This all belongs to Mr. Kendrick—and you two are over here begging and pestering. And you let Bounce follow you over to beg.

BONNIE

Mr. Kendrick said we could get something to eat.

STEW

He said we could have a candy, too.

BONNIE

Molly, we're hungry.

MOLLY

Oh, get your tails into the house. That is Mr. Kendrick's house, so you behave yourselves.

[Fade to] . . .

(Late afternoon. The twins, Bonnie and Stew, come tumbling out of the house, their cheeks bulging with peppermint candy)

MOLLY

Now I'm going to take you skinks home. And hope to God Dad doesn't find out you've been begging the neighbor for food.

(They all look over in surprise at the barn, where Thomas has emerged, leading the horses and his wagon)

THOMAS

(He seems reserved, thoughtful)

How about I drive you home today?

MOLLY

What?

THOMAS

I'll drive you and the twins home in the wagon. I want to speak to your folks.

(A sinister silence as Thomas climbs into the wagon)

MOLLY

(Whispering savagely at the twins)

Now you did it! I told you not to be wandering down here begging a meal. I might even get fired from my job.

STEW

No, you won't. Mr. Kendrick likes you.

BONNIE

I think he likes you a lot.

MOLLY

Oh, shut up. He's going to talk to Mom and Dad, and that might be a whipping for you two.

(Bounce gallops up, still clutching the hambone in his teeth. The twins load the dog into the wagon; then climb in, exchanging scared looks.

\Molly climbs up next to Thomas)

BONNIE

Molly, are we in trouble?

MOLLY

(To Thomas):

They won't come around again. They were just hungry.

(Thomas looks at her in surprise)

Dad'll whip the tar out of them if he finds out they been begging food. Dad likes to call himself a proud man.

THOMAS

(Studying her)

Is he?

MOLLY

Not truly. If you need to be proud, I figure you should do things to be proud of. Anyway, they won't come around for food anymore. Dad'll get pretty mad.

THOMAS

Ah. Well, I want to speak to your mother too.

MOLLY

About what?

STEW

Are you going to tell on us, Mr. Kendrick?

THOMAS

I won't tell unless I'm asked. Then I might have to make up some kind of lie. You can come over and visit anytime you want. Bounce can come too. I like the company.

(Thomas drives the wagon into the squalid, dirt-poor Simmons farm. He jumps down from the wagon)

I'll only be a little while.

(Molly watches him go up to the house. Her mother Maude answers, with a look of surprise, then ushers him inside. Molly wanders into the yard, but her eyes glance continuously at the house. Suddenly her mother appears on the back porch and yells out):

MAUDE

(Her voice like gunshots in the quiet evening)

Earl! Earl, come up here!

(The twins gather round Molly as they watch their father trudge up from the hog pens)

STEW

He's telling on us. Now we're gonna get whipped.

MOLLY

Be quiet, Stew.

(Earl Simmons, frowning at Thomas's wagon in his yard, enters the house. Molly wanders the yard, glancing in fear at the house. The twins exchange worried looks. Bounce lies in the shade, chewing his hambone. Finally Thomas comes out of the house, bowing respectfully to Molly's mother. He puts on his hat and strides across the yard to Molly. She watches him in fear)

THOMAS

(Seems nervous)

All right, that's settled! Now I need to speak with you, Molly.

MOLLY

About what?

THOMAS

(Glances around)

Not here. I kind of need to speak to you alone.

MOLLY

Alone?

(She looks at the twins, who stand staring—at Bounce, who pauses in his chewing to stare—at her mother who stands on the porch watching)

THOMAS

Over there, behind your barn. That should do.

(They wander down behind the barn, Molly's dress brushing him. The twins creep behind them, spying. Finally Thomas halts. He takes Molly by the shoulders, startling her)

Well, here goes. I'm in love with you, Molly.

MOLLY

(Her eyes grow wide in astonishment)

Oh God!

THOMAS

(Lowers himself to one knee. He draws a small ring box out of his shirt pocket)

This isn't gold, but it's solid silver. It's all I could afford.

(He opens the little box. A silver ring)

MOLLY

Oh God! Oh, My God!

THOMAS

I'm asking you to marry me. To be my wife.

MOLLY

Oh God!

(A long, shocked silence. The twins stare around the barn. Bounce wanders over to stare)

THOMAS

I know you're only sixteen. Your dad let me know that a few times. And I'm willing to wait—

MOLLY

You want to marry me?

THOMAS

Yes, that's what I'm asking—if you want to.

MOLLY

(Stares down at the ring. Stares up at Thomas)

[Fade to] . . .

(The poultry plant, present day, 1950. The sun darkens under passing clouds, then bursts bright in the sky. The wind blows mournfully across the prairie. Molly smiles at the memory, rubs the ancient silver ring, many times repaired, still on her finger. She looks across the expanse at Mr. Harrison spraying weeds and pausing now and again to prune the shrubs outside the plant office. No other human seems to exist—the windblown poultry plant seems deserted. Then the growl of a huge poultry truck driving into the plant. She watches it pull around the line of endless steel buildings and grind away)

[Fade back] . . .

(A crisp, windy evening, early November. The horses and wagon draw into Thomas's farm. Molly and Thomas have just been married. He helps her down from the wagon. She is wearing the sky-blue dress. They hug and kiss, then climb the porch to the house)

THOMAS

Hold it. I need to carry you across the threshold.

MOLLY

Oh, Lord.

(Thomas carries her inside, swinging the door shut with his boot. He sets Molly down and kisses her)

THOMAS

Well, we're home, my love. Now this place belongs to you. And me too, of course.

MOLLY

(Staring around the house)

I can't believe it.

THOMAS

You're now Mrs. Molly Kendrick. It's your job to make this house the way you want it.

MOLLY

(Looks around the house)

Oh Lord . . . (Glances at Thomas) . . . what do we do now?

THOMAS

Are you hungry?

MOLLY

(Glances in fear at his bedroom)

No. I'm not sleepy yet either. Thomas, Mom told me some things. But I don't know how to be a wife. What should I do now?

THOMAS

(Smiling)

You look kind of nervous.

MOLLY

I dreamed of this. But I don't really know how to be a wife. I don't know what to do.

THOMAS

This was a big day. You're not tired?

MOLLY

Not tired so as to sleep—in bed.

THOMAS

I'm not either. All right, here's what we do. Come over here and sit on my lap, lay back and get comfortable.

(Molly crawls into his lap, lies back against his shoulder)

MOLLY

Like this?

THOMAS

Yes, just relax.

(Molly begins to cry against his shoulder)

Molly, what's wrong?

MOLLY

It's my wedding night—I'm a bride with a ring—I'm a wife. I don't know what I should do. Mom told me about how babies are made . . . I already knew, but . . .

THOMAS

Stop being a worry-wart. We've got all time in the world to make babies.

MOLLY

Mom said that's what men want to do on the wedding night.

THOMAS

I don't know what other men want. I just want you to be happy on your wedding night—just that.

MOLLY

I'm happier than I've ever been in my life. But, Thomas, I'm scareder too.

(They sit and listen to the wind blowing outside the house. Thomas strokes her hair)

THOMAS

I'm scared too. We've both had a big day. We got married today, Molly.

41

MOLLY

We got married today . . . Oh Lord, I don't know. You'll have to tell me how to be a wife.

THOMAS

Oh no. I'm not going to tell you anything. I expect you to be who you are, and don't come running up to me to ask who you should be or what you should do.

MOLLY

(Smiling at him)

I love you.

THOMAS

I love you. And I belong to you forever.

MOLLY

(Looks at him, turning red)

I belong to you forever.

THOMAS

And tomorrow we're going to plant a tree to celebrate. I'm sorry I couldn't afford a Honeymoon, but for Our Honeymoon we're going to have to plant a tree.

MOLLY

Plant a tree?

THOMAS

And keep it well watered. It'll be a reminder that I need to one day take you on a proper Honeymoon.

MOLLY

We'll plant a tree. That's a better Honeymoon than going to Omaha or something. I'll get the tree growing, and we'll remember it.

THOMAS

I found it down on the creek bank, and I dug it up to replant. A burr oak tree.

MOLLY

An oak tree—here in Nebraska. Oaks grow slow, but sure.

THOMAS

They're an ugly tree, but a forever tree.

MOLLY

(Kisses him)

What kind of tree is that, my love?

THOMAS

It's a tree that if it takes off and starts to grow, will live long after any of us are on the earth. I don't know why that's important, but if we don't kill it replanting it, we'll have a reminder of our wedding day. And maybe our kid's kids will. It'll have to be kept watered.

MOLLY

I know how to plant trees and take care of them.

THOMAS

From what I've seen of you, Molly, you probably know everything.

MOLLY

(Stares away in sudden worry)

No, I really don't.

THOMAS

What's wrong?

MOLLY

Nothing. Just that there's things I can't do.

43

THOMAS

There's lots of things you can.

MOLLY

(Blinks her eyes, exhausted)

I'll be the best wife I can be, Thomas.

THOMAS

Are you ready for bed, Honey? You look sleepy—or would you rather talk awhile?

MOLLY

(Glances at the bedroom, tries to swallow a yawn)

I wouldn't mind talking for a while. What should we talk about?

THOMAS

Oh, what we want to do with this place, how to make a good living off it.

MOLLY

We've got plenty of winter food stored up. These drought years is—are—killing everything around here, but we've got water here. All it'll take is hard work.

THOMAS

(Stroking her hair)

When you climb that tall hill north of here, what do you see?

MOLLY

I see all those buildings going up in Lincoln.

THOMAS

It's growing like a weed. It's a city, almost over-night. That means opportunity.

MOLLY

I don't know much about that. (Glances fearfully at Thomas)—What I meant when I said I can't do everything?

THOMAS

Yes.

MOLLY

(Looks down at her hands)

I can't even read and write.

THOMAS

You don't know how to read, Molly?

MOLLY

(She looks away, in torture)

No, I never learned how to read and write. Dad said it was for people who don't have to work. I always wanted to learn, though, and I could. I know Louise Powers can read and write, probably pretty good.

THOMAS

I could teach you, if you want to learn how.

MOLLY

How to read? Yes, I want to learn how to read and write, more than anything.

THOMAS

More than your sewing?

MOLLY

At least as much, I guess.

THOMAS

All right. Then one evening we can spend you sewing and me reading, and the next evening we can spend teaching you to read.

MOLLY

I'll learn.

THOMAS

All right. Every other night we'll sit like this, and you'll learn to read and write.

MOLLY

I like sitting like this, with you.

(Looks at him)

Just because I haven't learned to read and write, doesn't mean I'm a stupid farm girl, like some people would say.

THOMAS

I love sitting here like this with you, and Bounce snoring on the floor.

[Cut to] . . .

(Bounce snoring and slobbering on the floor)

And with a little luck we can make a go of it here—find some way to squeeze money out of this dead farm . . . all of the farms around here are dying for lack of rain. So we have one thing, the creek. And a good well, now that we have the new pump from Omaha . . .

(Looks down at Molly, asleep in his arms, lightly snoring. Thomas gathers her into his arms and carries her into the bedroom)

MOLLY

(Jerks awake)

I'm sorry . . . I'm so tired . . .

(Thomas lays her in the bed and covers her up. He crawls in next to her and puts his arm around her)

I'm sorry, Thomas . . .

THOMAS

Molly, don't ever say that again . . .

[Fade to] . . .

(Thomas and Molly making love, groaning and crying under the covers. They climax, and Molly groans naked against him)

MOLLY

Oh Lord! You think we might have made a baby that time?

THOMAS

Only God knows that. But it was fun trying, wasn't it?

MOLLY

(Giggling)

Oh God Oh God, it was fun.

THOMAS

Oh, Lord it feels good to rest up. It feels good to be spent.

MOLLY

(Laughs)

It was fun. (She looks at him): Thomas . . .

THOMAS

Yes . . .

MOLLY

I been thinking about what we can do to make a go of this place.

THOMAS

(Looks at her in surprise)

You weren't thinking that while we were trying to make a baby, were you?

MOLLY

No. But it's been at the back of my mind.

THOMAS

All right, I guess. What is it?

MOLLY

When I went into town the other day, Mrs. Whithers at the store said she needed eggs; that people were wanting eggs, and fresh chicken. We put in chickens, we can sell chickens and eggs. Especially to the folks in Lincoln who don't raise chickens.

THOMAS

(Studying her)

Chickens and eggs?

MOLLY

In this drought we can't try cattle. We don't have enough cattle grass here—but we have room. And we have water. I raised chickens all my life, Thomas. We might try. We could feed a lot of chickens with only a few acres of corn and milo. And we could sell the eggs.

THOMAS

My love—(Spanks her lightly)—maybe we might. You were thinking that while we were making a baby, weren't you? (Spanks her again)

MOLLY

(Giggling)

No! I wasn't thinking anything then.

THOMAS

(Lies back in bed, contemplating. Bounce snores on the floor next to the bed)

Chickens and eggs . . .

MOLLY

Thomas, I wasn't thinking that when we were trying to make a baby. I wasn't thinking anything.

THOMAS

I wasn't either, my love. Now I am.

[Fade to] . . .

(Molly driving the wagon into town, delivering eggs and two chickens. Irene Whithers at the store in Denton, pays her a dollar and a quarter. Molly stares down at the money in her hand. Her eyes grow amazed)

IRENE

You bring eggs and chickens like this in here, Molly, and I'll buy them. Molly, these drought years is killing everybody around here. But Lincoln keeps growing, and they want eggs for breakfast and fried chicken for supper.

MOLLY

They're getting their beef cheap from the west. But they can't ship chickens very far. They can't ship eggs far at all.

IRENE

(Grinning)

There you go, Mrs. Kendrick.

(Molly, clutching the money in her hand, her mind swimming with possibilities, wanders the store)

MOLLY

I'd like to buy a couple of things with this money, Mrs. Whithers, if that's all right.

IRENE

You just get what you need, Mrs. Kendrick.

(Molly looks up as Louise Powers enters the store. Louise spots her and smiles)

LOUISE

Mrs. Kendrick.

MOLLY

Hello, Mrs. Powers.

LOUISE

Have you come to buy thread?

(Irene Whithers is gesturing at Molly—She's drunk!—try to ignore her!)

MOLLY

(glances back)

Some thread and cloth.

LOUISE

To make Thomas a scarf or something. (Stares away) . . . I shouldn't make such a public fool of myself. Some people have the courage to make the right choices—some people are just weak. It's strange that I chose cattle. Smelly, stupid things, but I chose them because they made us rich. Now in the drought, we're all going bankrupt. The price of things tumbles. Things you always depended upon. But you don't know what I'm talking about, Molly—do you?

MOLLY

Yes. You're talking about change. When things change, you have to change.

LOUISE

Well, Thomas got him a clever little philosopher after all.

MOLLY

I wouldn't be surprised if he did.

[Cut to] . . .

(A series of scenes: Thomas nailing chicken pens and a chicken house together. Molly shooing chicks out of the incubator and into the world. Molly driving the wagon into

50

town with straw-covered eggs and wood-caged chickens squawking. Thomas building chicken coops.

Dense, industrial music)

[Fade to] . . .

(The present, 1950. Molly stares at the plant, the wind-swept buildings. She looks down and picks up the first diary, opens it, and laughs at the writing. We hear her mind-voice reading the diary as we read it with her):

"This is the fust intry in my new diry that Thomas bot me. He said to rite everday in it, and I will. I will make my husband prod. If I rite here everday, when this diry is over I will see how good I got from here."

[The page fades. A winter night. Thomas bustles into the house with packages]:

THOMAS

Seventeen today! Happy Birthday, my love.

MOLLY

I'm seventeen today.

THOMAS

And here are your birthday presents.

MOLLY

Oh, what? You got me birthday presents?

THOMAS

You're only seventeen once.

(Molly rips open the first present. A bolt of sky-blue fabric and a brace of needles)

MOLLY

Oh, my God . . .

(She rips open the second present: a diary and three pencils)

This is a book you write in.

THOMAS

You don't have to start it until January First. Then you write in it what you did that day. It might be fun keeping a diary.

MOLLY

When I learn to write I'm going to tell all sorts of things to this.

THOMAS

And nobody can read it but you. That's the rule.

(Molly opens the last present. An illustrated children's book. The Red Chick)

You got me a book? Oh, Lord! Look at the pictures.

(She fingers the book, opens it and squints at the pages)

There's a lot of words to read.

THOMAS

It's a book that teaches you how to read. I know how much you like chickens.

[Fade—as Molly stares down at the book—to] . . .

(Early night. A fire dances in the crackling fireplace. Molly lies on Thomas's lap, the children's book open on her own lap. Crickets and frogs chirp and blow in the night. Coyotes begin cackling outside)

MOLLY

Those things . . . those coyotes.

THOMAS

No distractions, you're reading me a story.

MOLLY

They're out there trying to get into the chicken houses.

THOMAS

And they can't get in. Once they know it, they'll go away.

MOLLY

Bounce doesn't like the coyotes cackling. Listen to him growl at them. Good Bounce.

THOMAS

No distractions; you're reading us a story.

MOLLY

All right. (Takes up the book): So the red chick we-nt out to eat s—o—me eat some bugs.

THOMAS

You're doing great, Honey.

MOLLY

I sound like a kindergartener.

THOMAS

You sound like everybody sounds when they're learning to read. I sounded like that, everybody does.

Now keep going.

MOLLY

(Reading)

He fou-fou-nd lots of bugs—in the gar-den. That's wh-en the red chick saw all the vegg-e-e-ables . . .

THOMAS

Vegetables.

MOLLY

And that was wh-en the chick got into trow—ble.

THOMAS

Trouble.

53

[Scene fades with Molly reading from the book]:

[To] . . .

(Molly and Thomas sitting at the dinner table. She smiles at him)

THOMAS

How was your scouting trip to Lincoln with Mrs. Whithers?

MOLLY

We ate dinner at a restaurant on O Street. And then we visited some more. Thomas, we could sell chickens and eggs there, in Lincoln.

THOMAS

I think we should try.

MOLLY

Folks in Lincoln are wanting fresh eggs and chickens. I know how to raise fresh eggs and chickens.

THOMAS

And I can make chicken houses, and incubators. All right. Let's do it. We'll start a poultry farm. Eggs and chickens.

MOLLY

I told Dad what we might do, and he said we're crazy.

THOMAS

Your dad called us crazy?

MOLLY

He said putting all our money into chickens and eggs would lose us everything.

THOMAS

Did your dad ever once in his life take a chance—a risk?

MOLLY

Not that I remember. But what if it does go bad, Thomas? What if we lose everything?

THOMAS

Then we'll have to go back to drinking creek water. We're young and strong, we don't have that much to lose. I don't think it's complicated. All we have to do is get fresh eggs and fat chickens to the buyers in Lincoln, and we'll sell at a profit. It's a lot of work, but not complicated.

MOLLY

It might be, Thomas.

THOMAS

What?

MOLLY

I think I might have a baby in me.

[cut to] . . .

(A scream. A distorted, watery world in pink pain. A baby crunched agonizing to the world. Molly screams out in bloody horror. Voices echo from the mist):

DR. KRAMER

This was a bad one, Thomas. She's only seventeen. She might have been too young and frail to have a child. But she did.

THOMAS'S VOICE

Is she going to be all right?

DR. KRAMER

The baby's fine. But there was damage.

THOMAS

Damage?

55

DR. KRAMER

Thomas, you have a beautiful little baby girl. She seems healthy, and that's all you can wish for. Rebecca, you named her?

THOMAS

What is it, Doctor?

DR. KRAMER

There was damage. It's doubtful, Thomas, that Molly will be able to have any more children.

(Molly cries out of the pink hallucination: "No!")

THOMAS

Molly . . .

[Fade to] . . .

(Molly is lying in bed, in the house. Thomas enters, goes to her and hugs her. Molly cries against him)

MOLLY

(Wailing)

You heard what he said, Thomas! What the doctor said!

THOMAS

I heard what he said.

MOLLY

That I can't have any more babies!

THOMAS

Doctors are wrong all the time. You're too worried about the future. The future belongs to God, and you can't worry about it, Molly, because we have a little baby girl to take care of. We have Betsy to worrying about now.

MOLLY

Betsy . . . our girl.

[Cut to] . . .

(1950. Molly stares away at the wind. Mr. Harrison is carefully clipping the shrubs. She picks up the second diary, opens it. We read it with her, as the scene melts into the past):

MOLLY's VOICE

"I will shake when I write this, because there is a terrible blizzard outside, and I fear we won't make it . . .

[Fade to] . . .

(A raging blizzard. The wind blows snow hatefully against the world. There is only white chaos outside. Molly huddles in a quilt with Betsy in her lap. Molly is trying to write in her diary. She stares in fear at the white horror outside the windows)

MOLLY'S VOICE

"I am writing this because it may be the last thing I write. The world is dying out there. Nothing can live in that. The chickens are all dead, we can't keep warm in here. This thing is killing us all."

(The blizzard makes savage noises outside. Snow sweeps relentlessly on the blistering wind)

THOMAS

(Staring out the window)

I have to get out there and get some feed and water to them.

MOLLY

(Suddenly in the past):

Thomas, how can you do that?

THOMAS

One pail at a time.

MOLLY

You can't even see the chicken houses! Oh, God!

(She hugs Betsy against her)

This thing is going to kill us! If you go out there, you can't come back.

THOMAS

I'll tie the rope on. Come on, Honey. They'll survive if they get water and grain. All I have to do is get to them, and all you have to do is pump me buckets of water.

MOLLY

You're going out in that?

(They look at one another)

[Cut to] . . .

(The blizzard outside, the biting death-wind and blinding snow roaring outside. Thomas bundles into a long coat, rabbit-skin cap and a wool scarf. He ties a rope round his waist, then, carrying two buckets of water, plunges into the roaring blizzard. Molly runs to pump two more buckets; then she holds the rope and stares into the white blizzard. Betsy cries from her crib, and Molly glances back at her. She stares out at the blizzard. Bounce, lying in the corner, gives her a worried look)

[Cut to] . . .

(Thomas forcing his way, against the wind, into one of the chicken houses. He breaks ice out of the tin water troughs and pours fresh water. He looks down the long row of wooden nests. The chickens have gathered together in the run between the wooden nest boxes. Thomas has to bust with his boot the frozen lid of a wooden barrel in the corner to get to the feed. He takes a steel scoop and chomps it into the frozen corn and milo mixture in the barrel. He breaks apart the feed with his gloves. He begins scooping it into the feeding troughs. The blizzard wails outside. Snow blasts the wooden walls. He spies a few dead chickens, frozen in the corners of the chicken house. Suddenly the door swirls open and Molly, wrapped up in coat and scarf, brings in two buckets of fresh water)

THOMAS

Molly! Christ, what are you doing?

58

MOLLY

(Only her terrified eyes are visible over her scarf)

I brought you more water.

THOMAS

You need to get back to the house. You need to stay with Betsy!

MOLLY

Betsy's asleep, and she's bundled up. We got a lot more buildings of chickens to try and feed and water.

(She looks down at the frozen chickens in the corners)

Oh Lord. Are we going to lose everything?

THOMAS

No. If we can get food and water to them . . . after this thing blows over, I'll clean those dead ones out and toss them to the coyotes.

MOLLY

(Shudders, listening to the blizzard)

Is this ever going to be over?

THOMAS

It blew in fast, so it should blow out fast, and leave us trapped in the snow.

MOLLY

There's drifts out there I couldn't even walk through! I had to crawl and try not to spill the buckets.

THOMAS

At least we won't starve. We've got plenty of chickens and eggs.

MOLLY

Oh, God—I'm scared, Thomas.

THOMAS

I am too. But being scared isn't going to keep our chickens alive.

MOLLY

We should get back to the house. I'll make a big pot of coffee. We can get warmed up, then take care of the second chicken house. Then get back to the house and warm up again, and go out to the third one.

THOMAS

And so on. But we should tend to the last ones first. Get to the farthest building while we have daylight and we can get through the snowdrifts. Then every time we go out, it'll be closer to the house.

MOLLY

I don't think we have enough guide-rope to get to the far houses.

THOMAS

When we run out of rope, we'll tie it to the nearest chicken house. Then we'll only have to follow the line of buildings. We'll need the axe to break open the feed barrels. I had to boot this one to hell to get the lid off.

MOLLY

Everything's freezing—everything's freezing.

THOMAS

Not yet. Come on, we'd better try and get back to the house.

MOLLY

We'll have to take a lantern—two of them. But we don't need to carry water to them, Thomas. We just need to get them feed.

THOMAS

What do you mean, no water?

MOLLY

Thomas, when they get thirsty, the chickens will just eat the snow. I've seen them do it.

[Cut to] . . .

(Molly and Thomas, two wrapped and formless creatures, leaning against the horrid wind, struggling through the snow, sometimes crawling over snowdrifts on their hands and knees, holding onto the guide rope. They reach their house and struggle inside. Molly, covered in snow and ice, immediately checks on Betsy, asleep in her crib. Thomas adds wood to the fireplace)

THOMAS

It looks like we're going to camp out here in the living room. Too cold to try and sleep in the bedroom.

MOLLY

(Looks at her husband. Thomas is white as a polar bear. Snow glitters from his beard. His face is haggard, grey with worry. The wind and snow howl outside, and she sees that night is approaching)

I don't think we'll sleep much tonight, my love.

THOMAS

Molly, I have to go out there and feed those birds. We've put too much into this.

MOLLY

I'd better make us coffee. We don't dare wait too long to try and make it to the far houses.

THOMAS

You stay here and—

MOLLY

No, I'm going out there with you. They can eat snow if they're thirsty and they want to survive. But we can get them fed and hope for the best.

(They sit for a moment and listen to the awful blizzard outside. Betsy snores in a bundle of wool blankets. Bounce stares and shivers from his corner)

[Cut to] . . .

(Present, 1950. The diary): "I dint kno it til later on, but my littul brother Stew got a bad cold dring the blissard, and he died. I feel sick, looking out at all that terble snow.

Stew wuz a joy. That blissard—that dam blissard! It killed my littul brother Stew. Mom wont go on now, and Bonnie wont stop crying. Som day I mite read this and remember Stew, and how bad it felt when the blissard hit us."

(Molly looks away at the windy afternoon)

[Fade to] . . .

(A clear, frigid day. The farm is a white landscape of snow. Ten foot drifts almost bury the chicken houses. Molly carts a load of frozen chickens out of one of the chicken houses, carries it awkwardly across the snowdrifts, stumbling and growling, wading through the snow. She dumps the dead chickens, stares down sadly at them; then trudges back through the snow. Thomas exits another chicken house with a load of dead birds, carries them away into the field and dumps them)

MOLLY

(Calls out to him):

Dad said we might end up just feeding the coyotes.

THOMAS

(Smiles at her)

Did you believe him?

MOLLY

(Her voice comes out a cold white mist):

No, my love, I never did. But we lost probably a third of our stock. Some of my best laying hens are out there for the coyotes.

THOMAS

(Trudges up to her. His face is red in the cold, his beard sparkling with snow-mist. He hugs her)

Look out there at that damned prairie, all that snow. How many chickens died in that blizzard? How many cows and pigs? How many horses are frozen out there? How many folks couldn't or wouldn't try to save them?

MOLLY

(Staring at the desolate panorama of icy white)

I can't even imagine.

THOMAS

I might sound brutal, my love—but every chicken that died makes every chicken that survived that much more valuable. This all will melt away, and when spring comes we'll hatch eggs and make chickens and sell eggs.

MOLLY

(Staring at the white emptiness)

This will one day melt away, and it'll be warm again. But Thomas—could you build a sleigh?

THOMAS

A sleigh? Yes. What kind of a sleigh?

MOLLY

One that can make it into Denton with a load of chickens and eggs.

[Fade to] . . .

(The Whithers store in Denton. Molly trudges in, wearing a giant coat, scarf and hat, her face scarlet from the cold. An icy wind flows into the store as she enters. Irene Whithers smiles at her)

IRENE

Here's a little Eskimo, riding a sled into town.

MOLLY

(Grins at her)

Thomas built it. It works pretty good. I brought in some fresh eggs and some chickens to sell.

IRENE

I'll buy everything you've got. This blizzard killed near every chicken in the county. It may sound crazy, but when there's been a disaster folks want to eat a good fried egg.

MOLLY

I got a few of them out there in the sled. But this thing hit us pretty hard.

IRENE

When spring comes and this all melts and dries up, we'll take another trip into Lincoln.

MOLLY

I'd like that. We'll take a load of chickens and eggs with us.

IRENE

(Smiles)

And sell them to hungry folks for hard money.

MOLLY

For hard money.

(She looks over as the door blows open and Louise Powers enters the store. Molly and Irene exchange looks)

LOUISE

(Staggers up to them)

Ladies. Please put your eyes back to normal—yes, I have been drinking. Louise Powers has been drinking, let it ring out all the way to Lincoln—Louise Powers is drunk and ruined. Good day, Mrs. Whithers, Mrs. Kendrick.

MOLLY

Mrs. Powers.

IRENE

What can I help you with, Louise?

LOUISE

Nothing. (Studies Molly). You've ridden a horse-drawn sleigh here, through that snow, I see. In order to sell eggs.

MOLLY

And some chickens.

IRENE

(Uncomfortable)

Would you care to buy some poultry today, Louise?

LOUISE

No. I don't care for anything. (Studies Molly) I've been drinking, little girl. I've been drinking because this weather has destroyed me. It has destroyed Powers Ranch. There's nothing anymore but white death. This cursed Nebraska, giving us drought, disastrous storms, then white death. Nothing beautiful, everything tedious and ugly—I should never have stayed here.

IRENE

(Tentatively)

Did you lose a lot of your stock?

LOUISE

Stock? Oh, yes. Dead cattle frozen like statues out there in the snow. I can see them from the upstairs windows. Everything gone, dead under the snow.

MOLLY

How many of your cows made it through?

LOUISE

We can't know. We live with a husband too drunk to count his dead cows.

(An uncomfortable silence)

But you, Mrs. Kendrick. It seems Thomas got himself a pretty little Capitalist.

IRENE

(Embarrassed)

Mrs. Powers . . .

65

MOLLY

I don't know what that is.

LOUISE

A Capitalist, Molly, is a girl who gets up at dawn, bundles herself like a mummy, hitches horses up to a home-made sled and drives it into the town store in order to sell eggs.

Louise staggers back, almost knocking over a shelf. Molly glances at Irene, who slashes her finger across her neck and indicates with her thumb and index finger that Louise is drunk.

MOLLY

I'm selling chickens too.

LOUISE

(studies her)

A Capitalist never seems to have fun. Do you ever have fun, little girl?

IRENE

Louise, please—

MOLLY

I have fun sometimes.

LOUISE

I always try to have fun and pleasure. What is it that gives you fun and pleasure, Mrs. Kendrick?

MOLLY

I like to sew. And I like to read.

LOUISE

You like to read. So Thomas has taught his little Capitalist how to read.

IRENE

Mrs. Powers! Forgive me, Ma'am, but you're drunk, and I won't have you staggering into my store and—

MOLLY

It's all right, Irene. (Smiles sadly at Louise Powers) He's teaching me how to read, and I'm reading books. That gives me fun and pleasure.

LOUISE

(Tones of self-hatred)

Are you reading Shakespeare?

MOLLY

No. Not yet.

LOUISE

No matter, little girl. You're doing much better. You're making money. You're a strong and pretty little Capitalist, you'll do well.

MOLLY

At least now I know what it is.

LOUISE

(Studies her)

How old are you, Mrs. Kendrick, if I may ask?

MOLLY

I'm nineteen.

LOUISE

Nineteen. Building a business with Thomas. Raising a daughter. The American Prairie Girl, dedicating her life to work.

<u>IRENE</u>

Louise, maybe it's best you make it back home and try and get some rest.

<u>LOUISE</u>

Rest. Yes, that's my life, rest. You don't rest, little girl, do you?

<u>MOLLY</u>

Sometimes.

<u>LOUISE</u>

But mostly you work.

<u>MOLLY</u>

Yes, mostly.

<u>LOUISE</u>

Why?

<u>MOLLY</u>

When I work, it makes me feel alive.

<u>LOUISE</u>

And you get money for it.

<u>MOLLY</u>

And we give people food.

[Fade to] . . .

(The chicken farm. A rooster crows at the pink-and-blue dawn. Hundreds of chickens begin squawking. Yellow chicks waddle into the morning, peeping, looking for bugs to eat. Tired voices from the bedroom):

<u>MOLLY</u>

Oh, Lord. Listen to them out there. I'd better get up and get the eggs.

THOMAS

I'm too tired to move.

MOLLY

I'm too tired to think about moving.

THOMAS

Well, take some time off. Invite Lois over for tea or something.

MOLLY

Invite Lois over for tea?

THOMAS

Why not?

[Cut to] . . .

(Lois riding her horse into Molly's place. She gets down and Molly rushes out of the house to give her a hug)

MOLLY

You made it through the winter!

LOIS

Just barely. (Looks around her) Molly, you guys are doing good. You're really making a go of it. Look at your garden.

MOLLY

Come on inside. I made some tea and biscuits.

(They enter the house, and Lois looks around, impressed)

LOIS

This is a good house, Molly. I'm proud of you.

MOLLY

It's a lot of work. (Smiles at her friend) Word is that you're going to be married. The Ferguson boy.

LOIS

Bill Ferguson. He asked to marry me.

MOLLY

What did you say?

LOIS

I said yes, but I don't know if I should have.

MOLLY

What do you mean?

LOIS

It's not the same, Molly. You were always in love with Thomas Kendrick, from when you were 12 years old. When he asked you to marry him, did you stop and think about it, and not know what to say?

MOLLY

No. I was too shocked.

LOIS

Were you scared?

MOLLY

Oh, yes. I was scared to death.

LOIS

But how long did it take you to say yes?

MOLLY

About one second.

LOIS

My God, Molly. I'm scared of being married, of being a wife.

MOLLY

Word is that Bill Ferguson is a good man, a good hard worker.

LOIS

(Darkly)

Sometimes word is wrong.

[Cut to] . . .

(Evening. Lois rides away from the farm and Thomas trudges up from the chicken houses. Molly is preparing dinner. Thomas sits down heavily in the easy chair. He rubs at his aching muscles)

THOMAS

Did you and Lois have a good tea party?

MOLLY

Yes. She's thinking about marrying the Ferguson boy, Bill.

THOMAS

Bill Ferguson. All right.

MOLLY

You know him?

THOMAS

Yes.

MOLLY

You don't care for him?

THOMAS

No.

MOLLY

Why not?

THOMAS

Oh, I don't know. He seems lazy. I don't trust lazy people.

MOLLY

I hope she finds happiness. What makes you think he's lazy?

THOMAS

Molly, you can spot a lazy person as well as I can. I hope Lois and Bill Ferguson will have a happy life together and all that . . .

MOLLY

But you don't think so.

THOMAS

Do you?

MOLLY

I don't know. I hope so. She stared at our place, and she was longing.

THOMAS

What?

MOLLY

She was longing for what we have, what we're building. I hope to God she finds it.

THOMAS

It's not easy to find, out in this prairie.

MOLLY

(Watches Lois ride away down the road)

No, it's hard. That's what makes it better.

[Fade to] . . .

(The present, 1950. A truck grinds out of Kendrick Poultry Plant. Mr. Harrison waves to the driver. The day grows quiet again. Molly picks up another diary, reading it):

MOLLY'S VOICE

"Twelve June, 1900. Betsy turned fourteen today. Thomas bought her a colt for her birthday, a beautiful little paint, white-spotted-black. We've almost finished the two big chicken houses west of the house, and we are carting eggs and chickens into Lincoln and Omaha like my mind can't believe. America is growing like a weed, and we are giving them chickens and eggs to eat. I see money coming to us that I can't believe. Dad confronted me the other day, for money. Dad doesn't like that me and Thomas have made such a successful go of it:

EARL

Molly—you have money now—all right. As a daughter, you need to give some of that money back to the family. Stew's dead, that's all gone. But Bonnie's hungry, and you need to send some of your money back to the family.

MOLLY

What's Mom say?

EARL

Your Mom says what I tell her to say. I raised you, Molly, I got you survived. Now you owe the family what you can give. You and your man are making money, ever body around here knows that.

MOLLY'S VOICE (From the diary):

"Thomas and me are getting rich, that's true; but I mourn some around here who fell by the wayside:

"There was a tragedy the other day. Louise Powers murdered her husband, and then she took her own life. So many folks around here talked it up and said it wasn't a surprise. Mason had lost everything, the mansion, the land, the cattle, everything. I didn't like Louise Powers. She hated me and loved my husband. But in some way I admired her.

It should be that the tragic dead are left alone, since no one but them knows the truth. But there is always a lot of gossip and talk in this part of the country" . . .

[Fades with Molly's voice to] . . .

(A dark April night. The wind is stormy, and lightning flickers in the dark distance. Horses neigh and whinny outside, and Molly steps onto the porch, the wind blowing her hair wildly about. Three men ride horses into the drive. The county sheriff and two deputies)

MOLLY

(Calls to them):

We're going to get rain tonight.

SHERIFF

(Climbs down from his horse)

That we are, Mrs. Kendrick. I hate to bother you folks, but I need to talk to Mr. Kendrick.

(Thomas has stepped onto the porch. He stares at the dark, rumbling storm in the southwest. He touches Molly on the back)

THOMAS

Sheriff?

SHERIFF

Mr. Kendrick, we've got a serious situation over at the Powers place. We think Louise may have killed her husband, Mason? You know these folks?

THOMAS

(Shocked)

I know them.

SHERIFF

Well, Mrs. Powers is hold up in their place. She shot twice at my deputies when they tried to enter the place. I think she's drunk and crazy . . . and I think she killed her husband.

MOLLY

(Staring away at the storm)

Oh God . . .

THOMAS

She shot at you?

SHERIFF

I don't want any of my men killed. She's crazy, and she's yelling about you.

THOMAS

(Trades looks with Molly)

About me?

SHERIFF

She wants to talk to you—then she'll give herself up.

THOMAS

Louise—murdered Mason . . .

SHERIFF

We think so. She yelled out that if she could talk to you, she'd give herself up.

THOMAS

Holy God.

[Cut to] . . .

(Molly rides behind Thomas, their horses stepping into the dark storm. The Powers mansion stands like a white skeleton on her hill. Armed men surround the house, and Molly hears a frightening screech come out of a window of the house):

"I took the wrong road! Where's Thomas! I took the wrong road, and now I'm mad!"

(Thomas gets off his horse and approaches the house)

THOMAS

Louise! It's Thomas, I'm here! Louise, you need to come out!

LOUISE

Thomas, is that you?

THOMAS

It's me. You need to come out, Louise.

LOUISE

I took the wrong road, Thomas.

THOMAS

Where's Mason?

LOUISE

Mason's dead. Out of his misery. I took a very bad road, Thomas, so long ago. Goodbye.

THOMAS

Louise—

(starts as he hears a gunshot. He looks back at Molly, who stares wide-eyed from her horse)

Louise! Louise?

(Rain begins showering down, lightning flickers in the dark clouds)

[Fade to] . . .

(Mid summer. The sun blazes in a cloudless sky. Betsy is riding her paint over the prairie. Molly and Thomas are sitting on the porch watching her)

MOLLY

She's riding reckless. She thinks she's Queen of the Prairie.

THOMAS

(Smiles)

No, you're Queen of the Prairie. Why are you frowning so much?

MOLLY

That new contract with Worthington's . . .

THOMAS

I know. We might not make it, Molly. But all we have to do is try our damndest. We've done that before.

MOLLY

They want a thousand eggs a week, Thomas.

THOMAS

We'll build more chicken houses then. We'll buy more wagons, we'll hire more workers—we'll do it.

MOLLY

(Grabs his chin-whiskers and gives them a playful yank)

And if we fail? If we put everything into this and we can't make the contract?

THOMAS

(Grins at her)

Then we go back to drinking creek water. Look at Betsy out there, our beautiful daughter. We haven't failed yet, my love.

MOLLY

No, we haven't, my love.

THOMAS

Remember The Red Chick?

MOLLY

I do.

THOMAS

I loved that book. A great story.

MOLLY

I loved it too.

[Fade to] . . .

(Molly, at 17, lying on Thomas's lap, the fire burning in the darkness. Under lantern-light, Molly reads from her first book, The Red Chick):

MOLLY

And so the Red Chick gr-ew up to be a shi-cane . . .

THOMAS

A chicken.

MOLLY

(Blushes)

A chicken. And then the Red Chick we-ent out to the wor-led.

THOMAS

The world.

MOLLY

(Smiles, embarrassed)

The world. And the Red Chick saw so ma-ny th-ings . . .

THOMAS

(Hugs Molly and gives her a kiss) The Red Chick saw many things, didn't he?

MOLLY

But he's getting into trouble.

THOMAS

When you explore the world you get into trouble.

MOLLY

And I can spell trouble now.

THOMAS

I think our Red Chick in the book is going to do all right.

MOLLY

He's making a lot of mistakes, wandering around eating the garden.

THOMAS

Is he, my love?

MOLLY

I think so. But it's a pretty good story. I like the Red Chick.

THOMAS

I like him too.

[Fade to] . . .

(The year 1905. Kendricks Poultry. A colossal sprawl of chicken houses and wired pens. Wagons entering the farm to load chickens and eggs; wagons drawing out of the farm. Thomas standing out in the complex, directing the loading and supply.

Molly, in their office, sits at her desk, calculating revenue on a white page. Her office door skreaks open, and a well-dressed businessman enters)

MOLLY

(Feigns surprise)

Mr. Worthington! How nice to see you.

MR. WORTHINGTON

Mrs. Kendrick, it's nice to see you too. Your daughter Betsy is getting prettier by the minute. And so, I might add, are you.

[A quick fade] . . .

(Betsy, grinning pretty at a high-school play, her eyes seeking her mother in the audience. Betsy playing Juliet. Thomas next to Molly, his hand with hers)

[Back to] . . .

MOLLY

Thank you, Mr. Worthington. You're here to buy us out, aren't you?

WORTHINGTON

(Smiles)

Molly Kendrick, you are something. We know what you and your husband have built. Kendrick Poultry is an established name here in Nebraska. The name will go on, I promise you.

MOLLY

Have you spoken to my husband about this?

WORTHINGTON

Yes. He told me to speak to you. I believe he wants to sell. Our offer will make you rich beyond your years, Mrs. Kendrick. Your husband only wants the Kendrick label to stay, and that is agreed.

MOLLY

I see. You'll have our answer tomorrow, Mr. Worthington.

WORTHINGTON

Mrs. Kendrick. (Bows and exits)

[Cut to] . . .

(Molly and Thomas walking in the yard, the old farmhouse behind them)

THOMAS

I'm thinking it's probably time. Betsy wants to live in Lincoln.

MOLLY

I've never even imagined living in a city. What would I do?

THOMAS

I think it's time, Molly. I feel it. Time for a change.

MOLLY

I don't like change, Thomas. They'll tear our house down, all we built with our hands. They'll tear our house down!

THOMAS

Yes, they will. But there will never be a better offer, and that includes a lot of stock in Worthington. I don't like change either—but I feel that it's time for change.

MOLLY

I suppose I was thinking that too. Things are getting too big. (Looks back at the house) But Thomas, how can we let this go?

THOMAS

The same way we started it, with hope and backbone.

MOLLY

Living in Lincoln, in the middle of a city? What would we do?

THOMAS

Knowing us, I think we'll find something to do.

[Cut to] . . .

(A busy street in downtown Lincoln, the year 1906. Two shops side by side: Kendrick Dress Making, and Kendrick Carpentry. Thomas is making an ornate dresser with a young apprentice, John Erickson. Thomas takes and studies a drawer John has just crafted)

THOMAS

Good. Very good. I'm tempted to give you a raise for one reason, John.

JOHN

(Looks up from his work)

What's that, Thomas?

THOMAS

You're so good with drawers. The crucial test of the quality of a dresser. The carvings and basic structure are all well and good—but they don't have to do anything. The drawers have to open and shut perfectly every time. And by God you make good ones.

JOHN

Thank you, Sir.

THOMAS

Why are you so nervous this morning?

JOHN

Sir, I've invited Mrs. Kendrick over from next door. Here she is now.

(Molly bustles in the door that separates her dress shop from Thomas's carpentry shop. She smiles at her husband. He frowns back)

MOLLY

I've talked to John about this already, my love.

THOMAS

About what?

JOHN

Sir—Thomas—Sir—Betsy and me are in love, and we want to get married.

THOMAS

(Stares at him)

You and my daughter? What are you saying? You want to marry my daughter?

JOHN

(Very nervous)

Well, I'm saying that Betsy and I are in love, and we want to be married. I'm asking your blessing. Go ahead and fire me, if that's what you're going to do. But I'm in love with Betsy, and she loves me. I can make a good living anywhere I go—I don't need you or your money. I want to marry her, and I will, with your blessing or not. There you have it.

MOLLY

Well said.

THOMAS

No, it wasn't, it was insulting. Mr. Erickson, I trusted you. I took you in and taught you carpentry and was very close to giving you a raise in pay.

JOHN

Well, you'll have to take it as it stands, Thomas—Sir.

THOMAS

My wife and I need to speak about this. You have the rest of the day off.

JOHN

Does that mean I'm fired?

THOMAS

That means you have the rest of the day off! Now get out of here.

[Exit John] . . .

(When he is gone Molly and Thomas break into laughter)

THOMAS

Did you see the look on his face?

MOLLY

You were Shakespearean, my love. Only don't ever let Betsy know how you treated him.

THOMAS

The man wants to marry my daughter. I don't owe him any courtesy.

MOLLY

Well, I have to get back to the shop. And aren't you making a cabinet?

THOMAS

A dresser.

MOLLY

It looks perfect.

THOMAS

(Stares at her)

Molly, I'm scared.

MOLLY

(Stares back)

Of Betsy leaving. Going away with a husband.

THOMAS

Yeah.

MOLLY

I'm scared too.

THOMAS

Whether she's going to be safe—happy?

MOLLY

I know. It had to come. She was in love with him from day one.

THOMAS

(Laughs, startling Molly)

And did you see the look on his face? First I told him I was going to give him a raise, then he makes his speech, and he thinks I'm going to fire him. That was funny.

MOLLY

It was cruel. But it was funny.

(Molly and Thomas hug and laugh into one another's arms)

[Cut to] . . .

(Betsy and John's marriage. Molly, in a gorgeous dress of silver, stands with Thomas and watches her daughter blush and smile at the primitive camera that bursts blue smoke as it takes the photograph. The tall-spired church of the Presbyterians stands in the background. The city of Lincoln rises grey beyond)

MOLLY

God said I could only have one child, my love. But she's a good one.

THOMAS

(Handsome in his silver-black tuxedo)

Yes, she is, my love.

MOLLY

(Begins to cry)

I couldn't ever give you a son.

THOMAS

(Looks at her in surprise)

You gave me everything, Molly.

85

[Fade to] . . .

(The diary—With the images: "14 January 1919. John returned from the Great War. I never saw Betsy so happy or Thomas so proud. We had a party for him, Captain John Erickson. Lois came with her new beau, a fellow who seems good; a Swedish immigrant, Mr. Vandegrift, who has some land outside of Lincoln. Lois works with me in the dress shop, and often we talk about how we ran barefoot across the prairie and giggled and shared secrets. Amy is getting to know her father, after the years of the war. I rejoice at the end of the war. I see the boys returning from Europe, their eyes still seeing horror and terror. I see pride, but I also see a deep sadness. It is an American sadness. That alone makes this country the greatest that ever was. A deep pride, and a deeper sadness. How blessed I was to be born in America."

[Cut to] . . .

(A 1925 Ford lurches across the lawn of the Kendrick estate. Thomas is trying to teach Molly how to drive)

THOMAS

The brake, Molly! The brake! Oh, God—No!

(Too late as the Ford tumbles down a hill and slides down into the duck pond)

MOLLY

(Gripping the steering wheel, screaming):

Oh God, Thomas! This is a death machine!

THOMAS

Holy . . . ! You just drove our new automobile into the pond, Molly!

MOLLY

Will that hurt it?

THOMAS

I think it probably will. Good God, Molly, that's the brake, right there.

MOLLY

I'm sorry. But these things are dangerous. People shouldn't be driving around in things like this.

THOMAS

Good living God . . . (Shakes his head at her) We'll remember this driving lesson, won't we?

MOLLY

This is a terrible thing. It drove itself here into the pond. I couldn't stop it, Thomas.

THOMAS

Yes, you could. By using the brake.

MOLLY

I Told you I didn't want to try and drive one of these things.

THOMAS

Yes, you did, my love. And now we're in a duck pond. And our new automobile is probably destroyed.

MOLLY

Oh God. It ran us into the pond. Thomas, these things shouldn't be allowed.

THOMAS

Well, you might have killed this one, my love.

[WIPE TO] . . .

(The poultry plant, 1950. The windblown buildings of steel, the stark prairie beyond. Molly is tired. She picks up the last diary and opens it):

8 November 1934: "I might become a pretty accomplished writer some day. I see the cold snow and the wind out there, and I think I can write about it. How it fights you, and you fight back. A certain Madam Beveridge arrived in Lincoln from England, and she is giving a series of lectures down at the university. I had lunch with her, and she spoke of our American authors and what she has learned in her travels across the plains."

M. BEVERIDGE

You Americans work so much with your hands. Always this nervous energy I sense as I travel your nation, Mrs. Kendrick. Work is a religion to you.

MOLLY

I don't feel alive when I'm not working.

M. BEVERIDGE

I'm not sure that I approve of that much industriousness. But I admire it. Before I leave your city, I want you to build me a dress. Your skill is well recommended.

MOLLY

I would be delighted to build you a dress, Mrs. Beveridge.

M. BEVERIDGE

(Studying her)

What is it about money that so excites Americans?

MOLLY

I'm sorry . . .

M. BEVERIDGE

You and your husband are very wealthy. You no longer have to sew dresses. You could relax. Why can't Americans relax?

MOLLY

We don't know how to.

M. BEVERIDGE

You build and you build, and you never stop building. You build out here in the empty prairie. Do you not want to ever relax?

MOLLY

(Smiles)

No, not really.

[Fade to] . . .

(Thomas counting dollars at his desk. Molly enters and sweeps up to him)

MOLLY

My love.

THOMAS

(Kisses her)

My love. Look at this; I'm making money like a dog chewing a bone.

MOLLY

They're back from their vacation, John and Betsy and Amy. I think Betsy's pregnant again.

THOMAS

Oh Lord.

MOLLY

She told me she wanted kids.

THOMAS

I guess we do too.

MOLLY

(Hugs him)

This is going to sound stupid, my love . . .

THOMAS

(Gives her a look)

Good. I can't wait.

MOLLY

I look back at what we did. Mom dead, Dad dead, Bonnie married and living down in Georgia. Betsy with another child. Sometimes it just makes me scared, Thomas.

THOMAS

What does, Honey?

MOLLY

Oh, just how things go. Sometimes I don't know what to do.

THOMAS

(Kisses her)

Molly, I don't think there's anything you can't do.

[Fade to] . . .

(Thomas trying to teach Molly how to drive a car):

MOLLY

Oh, this damn thing!

(Slams the gear into first, the car screeching)

THOMAS

No, Molly. Slow and easy. Don't slam it into gear, work it into gear.

MOLLY

This thing will never be as good as horses. It can't replace horses, something as crazy as this, Thomas.

THOMAS

It already has. All right. Now let out the clutch—slowly! And keep your hands tight on the steering wheel.

MOLLY

I'll never learn this thing, Thomas.

THOMAS

You learned to read, didn't you?

90

[Fade to] . . .

(A diary page. We read the diary along with Molly's voice. It is her voice at age 60):

"Eleven October, 1935. I finally finished David Copperfield, and Thomas said he was proud of me, although he was a bit disappointed when I said that I liked our own Mark Twain better. Thomas sized the two up, making fun of himself as he tried on the accent of a snooty college professor. It was so good that I wrote it down as we were talking":

THOMAS (Age 67)

It seems to me that Twain—I admire him, don't get me wrong—was a belly-laugh writer, and Dickens was a secret-chuckle writer. It comes down to good taste, you know, My Dear Love.

"We were beginning to pretend to be snobs, and I always loved it so much":

MOLLY

If it's taste, My Husband, then it should depend on the taster.

THOMAS

I'm afraid, Mrs. Kendrick, that you're an ill-schooled American bumkiness.

MOLLY

And I believe you made up that word.

THOMAS

Dickens against Twain? Come now, My Dear.

MOLLY

(She smiles): My Love, to whom I belong forever.

THOMAS

To whom I belong forever. My girl who can never learn to drive an automobile.

"We got into a mock argument that I believe I won. I say that the American voice in literature is only now entering her adolescence . . . and maybe the British writers are into old age. Thank God we got a new shipment of books. If I couldn't read of a night, I'm afraid I'd go mooncalf. Well, Thomas went to bed early, said he had a headache, and I'll be joining him soon. I have some of the newspaper to go through first. I will never be able to drive well, those automobiles are too strange . . ."

(She looks down at the diary page. The page begins to fade. Molly stares away at the sunny, windblown clouds, at the poultry plant. It melts into night, and a snowfall. There is no wind, the snow outside the farmhouse falls gently onto the yard. It is the year 1886. The wood stove is softly hissing and crackling. Thomas is sitting on the leather sofa. Molly—seventeen again—lies on his lap, the first book opened in her own lap. The kerosene lamp burns yellow. Molly is struggling with her index finger to learn the words):

MOLLY

The litt—ul chick fe-lt diff—diff—er—en—Different!

THOMAS

Good for you, Honey! That was a tough one.

(She grins against him)

MOLLY

I love you.

THOMAS

I love you. And I belong to you forever.

MOLLY

I belong to you forever.

(They kiss)

THOMAS

All right, now, no more distractions. (Spanks her lightly). I want to hear the story.

MOLLY

(Embarrassed)

This is a little kid's story.

THOMAS

So? They're some of the best you'll ever read. Now go on.

MOLLY

(Squinting at the book, worrying her index finger over the words):

The litt-ul chick felt different, be—be—cows?

THOMAS

Because.

MOLLY

Because he was red and the oh—oh—thur chicks were—white.

(Scene fades with Thomas's voice: "You're doing real good, Honey. I'm proud of you" . . .

[Fades] . . .

Back to the diary page. Molly flips to the next page and we hear her voice as she reads):

"Today was a good day, but the wind was blowing a little chilly out of the north. That old winter is approaching."

(Molly stares down at the page in slow horror, as if seeing a dangerous animal.

We see the page again, the words.

Molly is paralyzed with dread. Camera pans down to her old hands holding the last diary in her lap. The wrinkled hands begin trembling. They can barely turn the page.

The page turns slowly over and we read the next page. No voice, only silence):

"My husband died this morning. I can write no more."

As we read the words, a teardrop strikes the page and a spotted hand wipes it off. The hand turns the page over. The next page is blank. The hand turns to the next page. Blank. The hand riffles through the remaining pages of the diary. All blank. Slowly she closes the diary and sets it away. The last book on her lap is The Red Chick, tattered and faded. She holds it up; then sets it away. She lifts a handkerchief and tries to wipe away the tears, but then she bursts into uncontrollable sobs, her old voice moaning in misery. She cries until she can't sit up in the car seat. She bends down, sobbing and moaning.

She takes deep breaths, gasping herself still. She sits shivering, trying to gain control. She takes off her glasses and swabs her eyes. She returns her glasses, makes a long, deep sigh, then looks out at the great poultry plant, the buildings and trucks, the endless concrete paving. She stares for a long while at the rusted stump of the old well-pump. Wind blows softly across the prairie.

Mr. Harrison is studying the car parked under the tree. All at once it starts up. He moans and cringes as it jumps fore-ward and almost collides with the burr oak tree. Thankfully the car jerks to a stop; then, after a painful screaming of gears, backs up, jerks and growls, then lurches toward him.

Molly gets the car up to him, and Mr. Harrison leans inside)

MR. HARRISON

Mrs. Kendrick, I would be honored to drive you home. One of the men can follow in a company truck to get me back here.

MOLLY

No, no. I'm getting the hang of it again. It's only a matter of trying to remember all these devices. I never was a very good driver anyway.

MR. HARRISON

Well, then—

MOLLY

But I only have to make it home in this . . . combobulation. That'll be the end of it for me and cars. You fellows should get rid of that old rusty pump out there.

MR. HARRISON

(Looks away at the pump) Oh, that thing. Yeah, we'll probably get to it . . . well, I hope you come back to see us again real soon.

MOLLY

(Staring at the farm): I'll never come back here again. You have a good day, Mr. Harrison.

MR. HARRISON

And you have a good day too. (Looks out at the windblown cornfield across the road from the plant). It's a good day to have.

MOLLY

Yes, it is.

(Molly drives away down the gravel road. Last theme music begins to play. Green fields of corn and grass sweep in the wind. Molly smiles at the day. The Packard drives away over a hill).

THE END.

SWEETIE . . .

(Animation)

(Rural Nebraska—1967. Theme music . . .)

A late autumn day in the countryside of Nebraska. Rolling hills, brown-yellow prairie, a green cedar grove, a cornfield whispering in the wind.

Teena Greene, 16 years old, is out taking a walk with her giant Newfoundland, Bugs. The dog lumbers next to her, snuffling at the prairie grass and wild plum thickets. A farmhouse is up the hill behind her a ways; the house where she lives with her father and Bugs.

TEENA

"Won't be long and it'll be winter, my big fat baby." She gazes into the wind, the grey over-cast sky. It is a dreary day, and her eyes are strangely sad.

Suddenly she jumps as Bugs gallops into the cedar grove and lets out a bellow. Teena runs over.

TEENA

"What is it, Bugs?"

She brushes the dog away from a red fox lying dead in the trees; it was caught in an ugly steel trap. Teena looks away.

TEENA

"Somebody's trapping on our land, Bugs. Dad's going to be out to skin somebody. No, stay away from this."

She kneels down to touch the fox corpse.

"You're—you were—beautiful. You were a vixen."

Looks at the trap.

"Whoever did this better hope I don't catch him. No, Bugs, stay away!"

Teena stands and stares into the wind. She wipes tears from her eyes

"She didn't have to die that way."

The big Newfoundland gives her a curious look; then stares down at the dead fox in the trap. Teena listens, hears something past the wind, a "Yip! Yip!" sound. She slips through the cedar grove, listening.

"Yip! Yip!"

Bugs barks at the sound.

TEENA

"Be quiet, Baby!"

Teena looks down at a mess of prairie grass covering a cavity under a big cedar tree root. Cautiously, she kneels down, Bugs standing protectively beside her, grumbling. Teena spreads the prairie grass away and peers into the root cave.

TEENA

"Oh . . ."

A baby red fox peers at her, its eyes wide in terror.

TEENA

"A fox pup!"

The baby fox cowers back, crying and whimpering.

TEENA

"It was your mom in that trap. Are you the only one?"

Teena pulls the grass away from the den.

"You are."

SWEETIE

"Yaii!"

Cowers into a ball as Teena reaches in the den to touch her.

TEENA

"You'd better come with me, Sweetie. You'll die out here without your mama. Come on, Sweetie."

Teena wrestles the baby fox into her arms. Sweetie struggles and cries out:

SWEETIE

"Aiii!"

TEENA

"No, settle down. I can't let you die out here all by yourself."

Sweetie, in Teena's arms, looks down at Bugs, a huge black monster, who squats and stares at her.

SWEETIE

"Aughhh . . ."

Hides herself in Teena's jacket.

TEENA

"Bugs won't hurt you. Settle down. Yeah, you lost your mom. Don't cry. I lost my mom too, a long time ago."

She carries the baby fox out of the cedar grove and up the path toward the farmhouse standing on a hill.

"I can't let you die."

[FADE TO] . . .

Teena carries the baby fox into the house, Bugs lumping behind.

TEENA

"Dad! Dad, I've got something here."

Her father is in the living room reading a newspaper. He gets up and joins Teena in the kitchen.

DAD

"What have you got there?"

TEENA

"A fox pup. Look at her."

Sweetie peeks out of Teena's jacket, whines and burrows back, hiding her face.

DAD

"Well, I'll be . . . a red fox pup. I've never seen one."

TEENA

"I found her mom dead in a trap. Somebody's trapping on our land."

DAD. (Scowls)

"Those miserable—they better hope I don't catch them."

Studies the bulge in Teena's jacket.

"What do you plan to do with that thing?"

TEENA

"It's a she. It's a little girl fox. I want to keep her, Dad. Please."

DAD

"Teena, that's a wild animal."

TEENA

"She's just a baby. I couldn't let her die out there alone and afraid."

DAD

"No, I guess not. She's probably hungry. I don't know if she's been weaned; I don't know anything about red foxes. Take her into the living room and keep Bugs away from her. I'll warm up some milk and you can try a calf bottle on her."

TEENA

"Thank you, Dad."

She carries the fox into the living room and releases her. Sweetie immediately scampers away and hides behind the living room curtains.

"Nobody's going to hurt you. Are you hungry?"

Sweetie peeks out of the curtains, ducks back.

SWEETIE

"Ahhhh . . ."

TEENA

"Bugs, you be nice to her. She's just a baby, and she's scared."

Bugs is staring, his head cocked, at the bulging curtain.

Dad comes in with a calf bottle filled with milk. Hands it to Teena.

DAD

"Well, good luck. I'm off to bed. I hope the thing survives. Don't you stay up too late."

TEENA

"I won't. 'night, Dad."

She gently draws apart the curtain, exposing Sweetie, who pouts in fear.

"Nobody's going to hurt you. Come on out. I've got milk!"

Teena dribbles some milk onto the floor, and Bugs thumps over to quickly lap it up.

<u>SWEETIE (looking at Bugs)</u>

"Ahhhhh . . ."

<u>TEENA</u>

"Come on, I'll take you into my bedroom, we'll get away from Bugs. You need to eat. Come on now, Sweetie."

She gathers the fox into her arm and lets Sweetie sniff at the nipple on the calf bottle. Teena takes the fox baby into her bedroom and lies down in bed with her.

"Now drink this milk."

Sweetie begins gobbling at the bottle Teena holds, cradling her.

"That tastes good, doesn't it?"

She pets the fox as Sweetie gobbles down the whole bottle. Sweetie burps, licks the milk off her chin, snuggles against Teena. Then she jumps up and hides in the covers. Bugs has padded into the bedroom. Sweetie lets out a cry as Bugs jumps onto the bed, causing it to groan. Bugs stretches out on Teena's right side. She rubs his face as he stares at the moving lump under the covers.

<u>TEENA</u>

"Oh, you, my big fat baby. This is Sweetie, and she's just a baby, so you be nice to her."

Bugs drapes his great head over Teena's stomach. Sweetie blinks out of the covers.

<u>SWEETIE</u>

"Ahhh!"

Bugs thumps his tail on the bed and Sweetie ducks back down under the covers.

<u>TEENA</u>

"It's okay. Bugs isn't going to hurt you."

Sweetie peeks out of the covers at Bugs, who eyes her with lazy curiosity.

<u>SWEETIE</u>

Yiiii?"

104

TEENA

"Oh, don't cry, little baby. Bugs won't hurt you, he wants to makes friends, see? Bugs is good."

Sweetie creeps out of the covers and approaches Bugs, who is still draped over Teena. Her eyes are wide staring at the giant dog. She sniffs at his nose, and Bugs thumps his tail. Sweetie ducks back under the covers, then cautiously peeks out. She creeps up to Bugs again, and he gives her a big lick of the tongue. Sweetie yowls and ducks back. Teena laughs. Sweetie ventures out of the covers and once again approaches Bugs, who gives her another lick. This time Sweetie fox-giggles, swipes him back, playfully nips at him. Bugs gives her a tired sigh. Sweetie crawls down, snuggling against Teena, and goes to sleep. Teena rubs Bugs and cradles Sweetie.

TEENA

"You guys are going to be good friends."

Wind blowing in the cedar trees . . .

[FADE TO] . . .

Time has passed. This is a montage of scenes to the song "Georgy Girl":

1. Sweetie fox-grinning, then galloping across the kitchen floor to attack Bugs, who is guarding his food bowl. They play, Sweetie jumping on top of him, then Bugs grabbing her in his huge paws and holding her down while he gives her a tongue bath.
2. Sweetie playing with Teena.
3. Sweetie next to Bugs as they eat. Two bowls, labeled, Bugs and Sweetie. Sweetie grins at Teena as she munches her puppy chow.
4. "You're always window shopping . . ." Sweetie curled up with Bugs and Teena. Bugs hugs the fox baby with his giant paw.
5. Teena working in the garden, while her Dad is in the distance working the fields on his antique John Deere B tractor.

As the song fades, Bugs sets up a bark. Sweetie yips in alarm. Teena looks up from her work. A Ford 150 pickup pulls into their drive. She smiles and brushes her hair away, leaving a dirt smudge on her cheek. She watches Chad York drive in, a boy who lives on the next farm over. As Bugs clumps barking toward the truck, Teena gets up and wanders over.

Chad gets out. He is a handsome young man who wears work boots, dusty jeans, a flannel shirt and a straw cowboy hat. He squats down to give Bugs a rub.

CHAD

"Oh, Bugsy, you big monster. Here, let me give you a rub."

Looks up and smiles at Teena.

"Hi, Teena."

TEENA

"Hi, Chad. What are you up to?"

CHAD (smiles at the smudge on her cheek)

"I had to pick up some supplies from town. Thought I'd stop by to see how you're doing."

TEENA

"Getting the cows in. They say we could have a blizzard tomorrow night."

CHAD (staring into the north wind as he pets Bugs)

"It's coming in. I can smell snow on the wind. You guys have plenty of supplies?"

TEENA

"I hope so. I guess here comes winter."

CHAD

"I heard you adopted a fox cub, and I wanted to see it."

TEENA

"She's Sweetie. She's hiding behind Bugs. Come on out, Honey, Chad's a good guy, he won't hurt you."

Sweetie peeks cautiously over Bug's back.

CHAD

"Hello, Sweetie. A red fox. I'll be."

He lets Sweetie sniff his fingers. She jumps onto Bug's back, fox-grins and lets Chad rub her face and back.

"I know, I don't smell so good. I've been working."

TEENA

"I don't smell so good either." (frowns in embarrassment)

CHAD (smiles at her smudged face)

"I guess when you work, sometimes you don't smell so good. Oh, you're a good little fox."

He tickles Sweetie, who fox-giggles and nips at him.

TEENA

"No, she's not. She steals Bug's food just for fun."

CHAD

"That's a fox for you."

He stands up, smiles at Teena. Looks out at the field where Dad is working to attach a snow plow to the tractor.

"Well, I can't stay long. I guess I stopped by for another reason. You've heard about the Monsterfest they're going to be showing down at the Grand?"

TEENA (blushes)

"Frankenstein, The Werewolf and Dracula. Folks are in arms about that. It might corrupt the youth."

CHAD

"That's why we should go see it. Three horror films for the price of one?"

Teena shyly brushes back her hair, making the cheek stain worse.

"Would you maybe want to go see it with me? It'll be there in a week."

TEENA

"You're asking me to the Monsterfest?"

<u>CHAD</u>

"Why not? I'll pay for the tickets and cokes and popcorn. You want to go?"

<u>TEENA</u>

"Yes. But I'll have to ask my dad. Have you been to the library lately?"

<u>CHAD</u>

"No, but we should go, when we can. I just finished Call of the Wild."

<u>TEENA</u>

"I haven't read that one yet. I'm working on Wuthering Heights."

<u>CHAD</u>

"So, if the roads don't snow shut, I'll pick you up and we'll head into the library."

<u>TEENA</u>

"Good. I have overdue books. Miss May's going to give me a lecture."

<u>CHAD</u>

"I always have overdue books. Somehow she seems to forget about them. Anyway, think about the Monsterfest. Three horror movies—it should be fun."

<u>TEENA</u>

"It's good to see you, Chad."

<u>CHAD (smiles at her)</u>

"Bye, Teena."

Teena watches his truck drive away. Sweetie is standing grinning at her.

"Guess what, Sweetie: I think I just got asked on a date!"

[FADE TO] . . .

A grey, overcast evening. The north wind brings light snow across the farm. Bugs is in the living room, sprawled out lazily on the floor. Teena sits on the couch reading a book. Sweetie trots to the middle of the hardwood floor, trades looks with Bugs who is looming over his food bowl; then glances up at Teena. Sweetie squats down and abruptly begins peeing on the floor. Bugs stares up in shock. Teena glances up from her book.

Sweetie finishes peeing; then dances away from the puddle, looking down at it. She glances up at Teena.

TEENA

"Oh, no!" (slams shut her book) "You bad fox! You don't potty on the floor!"

SWEETIE

"Yiiii!!"

Sweetie runs and hides behind the curtains. Teena puts her book down and gets up to clean the mess.

TEENA

"It's okay, you don't know any better. But you don't pee on the floor. You watch Bugs; when he has to go, he goes out the dog door. I'll have to show you how to use the dog door."

Sweetie peers fearfully out of the curtain. Teena goes into the kitchen to get a paper towel. When she returns to the living room, Sweetie has crept out and is playing with Bugs, biting his neck.

"I'm going to clean this up; then we'll teach you how to use the dog door."

Sweetie, knowing she is still in trouble, hides behind Bugs. Teena cleans up the pee, washes her hands in the kitchen, returns to the living room.

"It's okay. You didn't know any better. Come on and give me a love, Sweetie."

Sweetie creeps out from behind Bugs, scampers over to Teena and snuggles, pouting in her arms. Bugs gets up and lumbers over to the dog door.

"Now watch Bugs. He has to go potty. See what Bugs does."

Sweetie watches the big dog duck under the dog flap and go outside. She cocks her head in curiosity; then scampers over to inspect it.

TEENA

"Go on out. That's how you go out when you have to potty."

Sweetie sniffs at the dog-flap, ventures her head outside.

SWEETIE

"AH!"

She beholds the outdoors, and a candy-colored sunset. The wind is picking up, and she stares fascinated at the sparkling snowflakes that are beginning to dance across the yard.

TEENA

"Go on out, Sweetie."

The fox baby creeps out the dog door and stands on the porch, fascinated. She looks over to see Bugs lying on the porch, watching the snow.

SWEETIE

"Yiiii!"

She scampers over and attacks him. Bugs plays with her, then holds her down on the porch and cleans her face. Sweetie fox-giggles.

TEENA

"Look, Sweetie! See where I am." (Teena is poking her head out the dog door).

"Oh, look at the snow."

Sweetie scampers over to her, and Teena ducks back into the house.

"Now, come here, Sweetie. I'm in here."

Sweetie sniffs the dog door; then ducks under the flap. She runs into Teena's arms, grinning with joy.

"That's how you do it when you need to go outside to potty. Go on, try it again, I'll follow you."

Teena crawling behind her, Sweetie goes out the door and immediately attacks Bugs. Teena crawls out onto the porch, stares into the wind and snow.

Her father, trudging across the yard, calls to her:

DAD

"Teena, you'd better help me load in some more firewood for the stove. We might lose power in this thing."

TEENA (jumps up from the porch)

"I'll get my coat."

DAD (staring into the snowy north wind)

"Yeah, it's going to be a bad one."

[FADE TO] . . .

A dark winter night. Blistering wind sweeps across the farm, piling snow against the trees and fences and the cedar trees. Teena lies in bed, snuggled up with Sweetie and Bugs. The three of them listen to the gale that makes the window panes shudder.

A knock on her bedroom door. Sweetie jumps and stares. Dad opens the door; he is holding a flashlight.

DAD

"Well, we've lost power. You'd better get your quilt and pillow and move to the living room next to the stove."

TEENA

"I wonder if the school bus will get through."

DAD

"Ha. Look out that window, Teena."

Teena gets out of bed, shivers and parts her bedroom window curtain. She stares into a shrieking white world, cold and desolate.

TEENA

"We need to drain the water pipes."

DAD

"I did that already. Now get in there and sleep on the couch. We'll need to check on the livestock in the morning. You won't be going to school for a couple of days."

111

Teena makes a nest on the couch. The living room is pitch dark, only the slight cherry glow of the wood burning stove. Teena pulls Bugs and Sweetie around her on the big couch. They listen to the howling wind.

[FADE TO] . . .

The wind has died. Teena creeps off the couch and looks out the living room window. Snow covers the farm, a glittering world under the bright cold sun.

[CUT TO] . . .

Teena is hauling bales of alfalfa with her father over to the corral, where the cows have gathered. She strips twine off the bales and hangs it onto a fencepost. She breaks open the bale and spreads it out in the cow feeder, the cows bawling and nudging to get into the feeder, their breaths steamy and sticky in the icy air.

Bugs lets out a bellow. Sweetie, playing in the snow, yips and looks down the drive. Chad's pickup, a snow plow attached to the front of it, pulls into their drive, plowing a path.

DAD

"Well, somebody's out in this."

TEENA

"It's Chad."

DAD (wryly)

"Yeah, Teena; I know who it is."

Chad shuts off his truck and gets out. He's dressed in coveralls and a sheepskin coat. A wool scarf is wrapped under his cowboy hat.

CHAD

"Cold out this morning. Hello, Mr. Greene. Hi, Teena."

DAD

"What brings you out on a morning like this?"

<u>CHAD</u>

"I'm scooping the roads and some drives. Twenty bucks a drive and over 100 from the county."

<u>DAD</u>

"So I owe you twenty dollars?"

<u>CHAD</u>

"No, Sir. I just plowed in here to check on you. You don't owe me anything."

<u>DAD</u>

"Good, because I can plow my drive with the John Deere."

<u>CHAD</u>

"I just wanted to check in on you, see if you need any help feeding the cattle." (looks at Teena)

<u>DAD</u>

"My daughter tells me that you asked her out to those monster movies they're going to be showing in town."

<u>CHAD</u>

"Yes, Sir. With your permission."

<u>DAD</u>

"Okay, have fun and don't get too scared."

<u>TEENA</u>

"We won't, Dad."

<u>CHAD (smiling at Bug's snow-covered face,
at Sweetie squirming and playing in the drifts)</u>.

"I'd like to help you feed and water those cattle. I'm done plowing for the day. My truck's starting to overheat."

DAD

(gives Chad a grim eyeball) "You'd better not let that happen."

TEENA

"You should take a break, Dad. Go in and get some coffee."

DAD (taking the hint)

"O . . . kay. I'll go in and stoke the stove and warm up. Did you folks lose power, Chad?"

CHAD

"Yes, we did."

DAD (giving Teena a look)

"Well, I'll leave you guys to feed and water the cattle."

Dad wades the snow to the house. Teena pulls a bale of alfalfa, sled-like over to the corral. Chad hefts a bale and carries it over. They work awhile, Sweetie and Bugs romping around them in the snow.

CHAD (spreading alfalfa out to the cows)

"They're going to need water. Where's your ax?"

TEENA

"Over there, next to the fencepost."

Chad takes up the ax, crawls into the corral, brushing the cows away, and begins chopping the cattle tank, tossing shards of ice over the fence where they crack and clatter. The cows bully in to drink. Chad climbs out of the corral, stands with Teena.

CHAD

(takes off his wet gloves) "Well, at least we didn't have to go to school today. And we're going to the Monsterfest this next Friday."

TEENA

"If we can make it into town."

CHAD

"Oh, we'll make it."

TEENA

"It'll be fun."

CHAD

"It will be. Then next week we'll get to the library." (stares out at the cold, white prairie) "Pretty ugly out there, isn't it?"

TEENA

"No, it's beautiful."

CHAD

"Beautiful. What do you mean? The only place uglier than Nebraska might be Kansas."

TEENA

"I mean that Nebraska is beautiful because it's not beautiful."

They look out at the cold, desolate aftermath of the blizzard.

CHAD (glances back at the house)

"I'd—I guess I'd like to do something . . . but I need your permission . . ."

TEENA (looks at him)

"What's that?"

CHAD

"Well, Teena, I'd like to kiss you—with your permission . . ."

TEENA (blushing, looks down at Sweetie, sugared in snow)

"What?"

CHAD

"Well . . . if it's okay—I want to kiss you. Can I?"

TEENA

"Yes."

They hug and kiss. Then Teena looks down at Bugs and Sweetie, who squat in the snow giving her identical curious looks, their heads tilted.

CHAD

"I don't know if I'm any good at kissing—"

TEENA

"Kiss me again."

[FADE TO] . . .

Later that night, Teena and her Dad eat a cold supper under the light of a Coleman lantern in front of the wood-burning stove.

DAD

"You like that boy—the York boy."

TEENA

"Yeah, I like Chad. He's a . . . good friend."

DAD

"He's a hard worker, I'll give him that. They say he reads a lot."

TEENA

"He likes books."

DAD

"Well, you've got that in common."

TEENA (avoiding eye contact)

"This movie, Dad . . . The Monsterfest."

DAD

"What about it?"

TEENA

"It's my first date."

DAD

"Ah."

TEENA

"Three movies, and all the kids from school . . . and going with a boy."

DAD

"Aren't you excited?"

TEENA

"I'm excited. But, Dad, I'm scared."

DAD (pets Sweetie, who is sniffing at his plate of cold food)

"This little fox would steal my food the first chance she got. I had no idea foxes were such natural thieves." Looks at Teena. "I wish your mom could be here to talk to you about it. My God, it's been fifteen years . . . and I sure don't know what to tell you. Chad seems to be a decent kid. If he's not, I'll kill him. I think your best bet on this is just to have fun, and don't worry about it. You worry too much. Maybe you read too much."

TEENA

"You worry a lot too, Dad."

DAD

"Yeah, but I read the newspaper."

[FADE TO] . . .

A yellow school bus rumbles down a corridor of snow and turns into the high school. Teena gets out, hefting her books. Bill Snyder stands waiting for her, wearing his letter jacket. He is on the football team, and his father owns several businesses in Mars City. He is popular with the girls and arrogant about it.

BILL

"Hey, Tee. You guys get power yet?"

TEENA

"We're supposed to get it back some time this afternoon."

BILL

"That'll be good."

TEENA

"Yes, it will."

BILL

"Well, hey, Tee—you're going out with me! What do you think about that? To the Monsterfest next Friday night. Everybody's going and I want you to go with me."

TEENA

"Uhhh . . . thank you for asking me, Bill; but I already have a date next Friday . . . at the Monsterfest."

BILL

"You—you already have a date. What do you mean?"

TEENA

"I already have a date. But I'm very flattered that you asked me."

BILL

"I like you, Teena. I like you a lot."

TEENA (a bit creeped out)

"Thank you. But I already have a date for the Monsterfest."

BILL

"Who is it?"

TEENA

"What?"

BILL

"Who's taking you to the movies?"

TEENA

"Chad York."

BILL

"Chad? The farm boy. Who didn't even try out for the team."

TEENA

"He can't play football; he's busy working on the farm."

BILL

"He's busy reading books. Chad's a bookworm, Tee."

TEENA

"So am I."

BILL

"Okay, I'll take Sandy Hays. Your loss."

TEENA

"Was that your truck I saw down by the creek, on our land?"

BILL

"What are you talking about?"

TEENA

"If you're setting up traps along the creek on our land—then stop it."

BILL (laughs)

"I'll set my traps anywhere I want. You know what a red fox pelt brings at the Hide Store?"

TEENA

"I don't know and I don't care."

BILL

"Look, Tee . . . I didn't mean that. I know you have a pet fox. But I want you to know that I like you; I like you a lot."

TEENA

"If you like me, then stop trapping on my farm!"

BILL

"So, you're going out with the book boy, to the Monsterfest."

TEENA

"Yes, that's what I'm going to do. Have fun there with Sandy."

BILL

"I will. Hey, your loss, Tee. Watch out for your pet fox. It's going to start killing your chickens and stealing your eggs. That's what foxes do, you'll find out. And I have plenty of traps, and I know how to use them."

TEENA

"I have a double-barrel shotgun, and I know how to use It."

Teena marches away. Bill stands and watches her.

[FADE TO] . . .

Chad's truck pulls up to the public library in Mars City, which sits atop a tall hill of granite steps. The library is an old gothic building, starkly brown against the watery black-and-white texture of the town.

TEENA

"Since I was a little girl I've always thought of this as the Temple on the Hill."

CHAD

"And so it is."

Chad and Teena climb up the steps to the library. They're both wearing their work clothes. They enter, and Miss May, the librarian, looks over the top of her glasses.

MISS MAY (coughs)

"Ah, Mr. York and Miss Greene. You two look—sloshy."

CHAD

"Sorry, Miss May, we've been out in the fields."

MISS MAY

"It used to be that young people would dress up and clean up before entering a public library."

TEENA

"We like to call it the temple on the hill."

MISS MAY

"And so it is, Miss Greene."

TEENA

"And we didn't have time to clean up. You do close at six."

MISS MAY

"Thank you for reminding me. You see, I've only been librarian here for forty years. And you've returned all your books. Very good. I do see here, Mr. York, that you have accumulated an overdue fine of $1.25. That borders on the astonishing."

CHAD

"I've kind of been snowed in."

MISS MAY

"There is no such thing as being 'kind of' snowed in. I suspect that you're waiting for an Amnesty Day, and all your fines will be erased."

CHAD

"It wouldn't do me any good to deny that, I guess."

TEENA

"What are my library fines, Miss May?"

MISS MAY

(Checking her Rolodex) "Your fines, Miss Greene are exactly zero."

Teena smiles at Chad.

MISS MAY

"I might not announce another Amnesty Day ever again. A public Library operates on the principle that there is a difference between borrowing and stealing. But never mind, you brought your books back—late, but still readable. I would be willing, as always, to forget the overdue fines that you owe to the federal government—"

CHAD

"Thank you."

MISS MAY

"On one condition: You must read Wuthering Heights." (she trades smiles with Teena). "I know Miss Greene has read it, now you have to. Or pay the $1.25. I'll quiz you on it the next time you enter my library."

CHAD

"Uh . . . Wuthering Heights. I will, right after The Old Man and the Sea."

MISS MAY

"No, before The Old Man and the Sea."

CHAD

"I don't know, Miss May. Carrying around Wuthering Heights might get me beaten up."

MISS MAY

"Beaten up? Who would beat up a boy carrying Wuthering Heights?"

CHAD

"Her football player." (looks at Teena).

TEENA

"He's not my football player!"

MISS MAY

"What are you saying? What does a football player have to do with Wuthering Heights?"

CHAD

"A football player likes Miss Greene, and I'm jealous. She might like him."

TEENA

"I don't like him! I don't care about Bill Snyder, I don't even like him."

MISS MAY

"Bill Snyder. I don't recall the name.

TEENA

"He's just a guy."

CHAD

"A guy who likes you. A football player."

<u>TEENA</u>

"Why would I want a stupid football when I have a stupid cowboy?"

<u>MISS MAY (coughs)</u>

"A good question. A cowboy who must swear to read Wuthering Heights if he's to get any more books out of My library."

<u>CHAD</u>

"I will read Wuthering Heights. I promise."

<u>TEENA (grins)</u>

"You'd better."

<u>MISS MAY</u>

"Good. Miss Greene, I hear you've adopted a red fox."

<u>TEENA</u>

"Yes . . . I found her. She's still a baby yet."

<u>MISS MAY</u>

"Bring the fox here the next time you visit. I'd like to see it."

<u>TEENA</u>

"A fox at the library."

<u>MISS MAY</u>

"Yes, and that black monster you call a dog."

<u>CHAD</u>

"Bugs."

<u>MISS MAY (coughs)</u>

"Yes, Bugs. Bring him too."

TEENA

"All right."

MISS MAY

"And Mr. York—Wuthering Heights."

[FADE TO] . . .

Monsterfest montage: To the song Monster Mash . . .

1. Teena getting ready for the date. Sweetie watches her preparing a bath, the fox tilting her head in curiosity.

TEENA

"Thank God we got the power back, you bad fox. Hot water!"

2. Teena, in blue jeans and a pink flannel shirt. Dad in the living room, puts down his newspaper and smiles at her.

DAD

"Don't you look nice. Three horror movies; I hope you don't come home scared to death."

TEENA

"Everybody's going to be there tonight."

DAD (smiles)

"You look excited."

TEENA

"I'm about to jump out of my skin!"

DAD

"Here, Teena, five dollars." (hands her a five dollar bill)

TEENA

"No, Dad, we can't afford that. Chad's paying."

125

<u>DAD</u>

"Well, then don't spend it. But you've got it if you need it. All the work you've done, you deserve it."

<u>TEENA</u>

"Thanks, Dad."

<u>DAD</u>

"Bring me home a box of Jordan's Almonds. You can't get them but in the movie theater."

<u>TEENA</u>

"I will, Dad."

<u>DAD</u>

"You look great, Baby."

<u>TEENA (smiles down at Bugs watching her, at Sweetie fox-grinning)</u>

"Thanks, Dad."

She looks out the window as Bugs bellows out and Sweetie yips, scampering out the dog door. Chad's truck is pulling into the drive.

[FADE TO] . . . Montage to the song "Monster Mash"

3. Chad's truck pulls into town and parks across from the Grand Theater. They walk hand in hand up to the theater, blinking neon lights and the marquee, MONSTERFEST. All their classmates are gathering, everybody excited.
4. Teena and Chad sharing cokes and popcorn. A black-and-white Boris Karloff Frankenstein appears on the screne. Teena screams out with the other girls in the theater, burrows her face into Chad's coat. He smiles and hugs her.
5. Above them in the balcony is Bill with his date. He stares down at Teena and Chad.
6. Dracula appears, and Teena screams out, hugging Chad.
7. The Werewolf appears on the screen. Teena screams out and hugs Chad.
8. They walk hand in hand out to Chad's truck.
9. In Teena's drive, they kiss.
10. Teena in bed with Bugs and Sweetie, both asleep. Teena, awake, looks out her bedroom window. She smiles.

[MUSIC FADES TO] . . .

Miss May sits in the doctor's office. She is waiting for the doctor, and she is gazing out the window at the town of Mars City in winter grey and white gloom. The doctor comes into the room. His face is neutral, but his eyes very sad.

MISS MAY (coughs)

"Well, Stanley, give it to me straight."

DOCTOR

"Stanley. You haven't called me that in years."

MISS MAY

"I always let you get away with checking out the anatomy books, even though you weren't of age. I'd hoped you weren't checking them out in order to see pictures of nude women. But if you were, well look where it got you."

DOCTOR

"I'm afraid that's exactly why I checked them out, Miss May."

MISS MAY

"Well, that's two pieces of bad news from you today."

DOCTOR (looks away)

"We both knew this day was coming."

MISS MAY (coughs)

"We did. How much time, Stanley?"

DOCTOR

"Not long. Six months. Maybe more; maybe less."

MISS MAY (after a long pause)

"Well, it's longer than I thought it would be. At least I'll finally be rid of this cough."

DOCTOR

"I'm sorry, Miss May."

MISS MAY (looking out the window at the winter day)

"Nothing to be sorry about. Many boys have checked out those anatomy books over the years."

[FADE TO] . . .

A mild winter afternoon. Teena stares out the living room window, watching a truck out on the county road past the cedar grove and along the creek. She goes and gets a pair of binoculars out of the desk drawer and trains them at the truck. She frowns down at Sweetie, who squats on the floor looking at her.

TEENA

"That's Bill Snyder's truck." (looks again into the field glasses) "He's setting traps! We'll see about that."

Teena marches to the closet, takes out her double barrel shotgun, loads it and pockets four extra shells. Sweetie and Bugs dance at the door, expecting a walk.

TEENA

"No, you two stay here. I don't want you stepping into a trap."

Teena carries the gun down the hill; when she approaches the cedar trees she sees a figure run out of the creek woods. She raises the shotgun to the sky and shoots two rounds. The figure gets into the truck and roars away. Teena breaks the shotgun open, takes the spent shells out and pockets them in her coat. She loads two more rounds and fires them at the pickup truck, but it is far out of range.

Teena wanders the creek side, finding a trap here and there, snapping it with a stick. She looks up as Chad comes striding down the lane, his cowboy hat pushed back on his head.

CHAD

"Teena, what are you doing out here? Your dad's worried sick, and he called me. He said you were gone, and Bugs and Sweetie are still in the house and he heard a shotgun go off."

<u>TEENA</u>

"I'm springing traps. I didn't want Sweetie or Bugs to smell the bait and step into one."

<u>CHAD (reaches her, gives her a hug. Says grimly):</u>

"Traps. What's the shotgun for?"

<u>TEENA</u>

"To scare away trappers." (she smiles at him)

<u>CHAD (smiles back, kisses her)</u>

"And I thought you were just a bookworm."

<u>TEENA (looks up the hill)</u>

"Oh, there's Dad. And Sweetie and Bugs are with him."

<u>CHAD</u>

"Go tell him to take them back to the house. I'll help you spring any traps we might find. They probably didn't set many."

<u>TEENA</u>

"He. It was Bill Snyder."

<u>CHAD</u>

"Bill Snyder. You've been scaring him off a lot lately."

Chad looks up the hill where Dad is walking down to them, Bugs clomping next to him, Sweetie scampering ahead.

"You'd better keep Sweetie and Bugs away."

<u>TEENA (trotting up the hill toward her dad. Grins behind him at Chad)</u>

"Book worm!"

<u>CHAD (grinning back)</u>

"Bookworm!"

129

TEENA

"Cowboy!"

CHAD

"Shotgun Teena!"

[FADE TO] . . .

Music Montage . . . "The Pink Collar"

1. Teena puts a brand new pink collar on Sweetie. The fox sniffs at it, looks up at Teena, smiles.

"You have to be on a collar and leash if we're going to the library. And you have a pretty pink collar."

2. Sweetie dances and plays with Teena
3. Sweetie parades her new collar across the living room, looking over smugly at Bugs, looming over his food bowl; who gives her a droll look.
4. Sweetie and Chad wrestling for an old sock, Sweetie growling and attacking it while Teena sits on the grass petting Bugs.
5. Music fades into . . .

A grey but mild winter day. Sweetie, led by Chad, and Bugs led by Teena climb the granite steps to the library. At the top of the long stone steps, Miss May is outside smoking a cigarette in front of the stone-columned temple. They all climb the steps up to Miss May, Sweetie staring around in awe.

Miss May tosses her cigarette into the snow, smiles at the odd group.

MISS MAY

"Over forty years and I never thought I'd see the day. Well, bring these creatures inside and take them off their leashes."

TEENA

"Off their leashes?"

MISS MAY

"They'll be all right. Now bring them in before everybody in town sees what we're doing. A red fox and a black monster in my library."

Teena and Chad take the dog and fox into the library and unleash them. Bugs follows Teena and Chad down the book aisle, sniffing at the strange place. Sweetie hides behind Miss May's desk, her eyes wide in amaze. Miss May sits down at her desk. She watches Chad and Teena getting their books, whispering back and forth:

TEENA

"You always have to get a Jim Kjelgaard, don't you?"

CHAD

"And a Jules Verne. You have a problem with that?"

TEENA

"I'm only getting two books; Little Women and Pride and Prejudice."

CHAD

"I'd rather read the Wall Street Journal."

Miss May smiles, then looks away, her eyes tearing up. She stares up at the big clock on the library wall and hears it ticking.

TEENA

"We know, Miss May, it's almost six. We'll hurry."

MISS MAY

"No, don't you dare hurry. The library closes when I say it closes. And today it stays open. I need the company and you have all the time in the world. You kids take your time."

A sniff alerts her; Miss May looks down from the clock and smiles. Sweetie is peeking at her from behind the desk, Sweetie's eyes wide. She cocks her head at Miss May.

MISS MAY

"A red fox puppy in the library. I never thought I'd see the day. Hello, little fox."

Sweetie ducks back behind the desk.

MISS MAY

"You don't have to be afraid of me, fox baby. Miss Greene!"

TEENA

"Yes, Miss May?"

MISS MAY

"What's the name of this fox?"

TEENA

"She's Sweetie. I'll get her."

MISS MAY

"No! You get your books. This fox is being good. Come on out, Sweetie, and let me get a look at you."

Sweetie creeps out from behind the desk, fox-pouts at Miss May.

MISS MAY

"Aren't you a pretty little thing, with your pink collar. Come on, I won't hurt you."

Sweetie approaches her, sniffs her fingers. Miss May begins rubbing her face, causing Sweetie to grin.

"You are a pretty little fox."

Suddenly Sweetie jumps into Miss May's lap, causing the librarian to gasp and laugh.

TEENA

"Sweetie! I'll get her."

MISS MAY

"No! Get your books. This fox is being good. Get your books, Miss Greene, and take your time. You have all the time in the world."

Sweetie settles down under Miss May's petting. Miss May looks down the book aisle at Teena and Chad getting their books, at Bugs lumping behind. She looks up at the big library clock on the wall. She smiles down at Sweetie in her lap.

MISS MAY

"You know, Sweetie; things could always be worse than they are now. But things could never be better than they are now."

[FADE TO] . . .

(piano theme music) . . .

A cold windy day. Many people have gathered at the cemetery, at Miss May's funeral. Teena and Chad, dressed in black, stand before the grave as the minister's voice speaks just above the mournful win d:

MINISTER

"Miss Eleanor May was our librarian for 40 years. For nearly half a century Miss May tried to get the folks—especially the young folks—to read. She never married, and bore no children . . . no, that's not true. She bore many generations of children. Children like me who loved to go to the library and pick out books. Miss May changed my life forever. She was . . ." (he stares off, shedding tears) . . . "She was more important than she ever knew. Teena Greene, who stands at this last place with Miss May, told me exactly who Miss May was and always will be. Teena Greene said that Miss May was the keeper of the temple on the hill. And that she was . . ."

Chad and Teena walk hand in hand away from the cemetery. It is a cold, overcast day. The wind blows in the cedar trees around the graveyard.

TEENA (breaks down crying)

"She never married. She never had children."

CHAD

"Yeah she did. She had plenty of children."

TEENA

"Where do we go now?"

CHAD

"I think she'd want us to go to the library. She's not here in this cemetery. She's there."

[FADE TO] . . .

Spring finally arrives. A warm, bright dawn. A montage to the song "Daydream Believer"

1. Teena wakes, stirring Bugs and Sweetie. She looks out her bedroom window. Dad is already in the field, plowing on the John Deere tractor.
2. Teena eating cornflakes while Bugs chomps his dog food and Sweetie gobbles her puppy chow, chewing and grinning at Teena
3. Teena brushing her teeth ("My shaving razors cold but I don't mind")
4. At chorus, Teena pushing a wheelbarrow across the lawn. She loads a bale of alfalfa into the barrow and hauls it over to the corral, breaking it open and feeding the cows.
5. Dad driving the tractor over the cornfield
6. Teena working in the garden as Sweetie gallops around and tries to play with her . . .
7. (pause in the music) . . . Sweetie wanders, exploring, into the cedar grove. Quiet; only the wind blowing. Sweetie sniffs at the world, grinning, steps further into the cedar grove. Suddenly she gasps and stares. A coyote lurks before her, its eyes glowing yellow. Sweetie cries out and scampers away, but the coyote is on her, grabbing one of her legs. As it drags her away, Sweetie squeals out. The coyote hesistates, looking at a disturbance in the cedar trees.
8. Bugs roars out of the cedars and leaps onto the coyote, throwing it to the ground. The coyote squirms away and sprints into the trees. Bugs stands like a bear for a moment, looks back at Sweetie, who is cowering and crying. He lumbers up to her, licks her leg; then lumbers back up to the yard, Sweetie scampering next to him, glancing fearfully over her back.
9. (last verse of the song): Teena is working in the garden. Bugs slobbers up and she rubs at his face. She looks at Sweetie, who is squatting, her face afraid, who keeps glancing behind her at the cedar grove

TEENA

"What's wrong, Sweetie?"

SWEETIE

"Yahhhh!"

TEENA

"What's wrong with Sweetie, Bugs?"

Suddenly Bugs barks out and takes off toward the drive. Sweetie runs after him, her eyes dancing fearfully at the cedar grove where the coyote was. Teena looks up, shades her eyes with a hand. Chad's truck pulls into the drive. Chad gets out, squats and rubs at Bugs and Sweetie. Teena gets up, smiles at him. Chad smiles back. Sweetie grins at Teena.

10. (chorus hits as . . .) Teena and Chad kissing against the colored evening
11. Dad on the tractor, looks across the field at them, shakes his head, pats the tractor.

DAD

"I didn't see that, Johnny Popper."

[FADE TO] . . .

A slow drum beat. Night. Dad quietly opens Teena's bedroom door. (Slow music chorus) . . . Teena is asleep, Bugs sprawled out asleep next to her, cradling a sleeping Sweetie in his giant paw. As chorus fades Dad smiles and closes the door . . .

[FADE TO] . . .

The last day of school, and everybody gathers at Valentino's Pizza to celebrate. Chad and Teena sit at a table, eating pizza and drinking Cokes. Chad looks at the teens crowded into Valentino's, everybody laughing and excited.

TEENA

"Last day of school, Cowboy."

CHAD (smiles)

"And now we'll really have to work our tails off."

TEENA

"You work too much anyway."

CHAD

"I love to work. It makes me feel alive. And you work too much yourself, Fox Girl."

TEENA (standing up)

"I'll go and get us more Cokes."

CHAD

"You're going to get two Cokes back through this crowd?"

TEENA

"Just watch me."

Teena worms her way through the crowd of her classmates, makes it up to the pizza counter and orders two cherry Cokes. Suddenly Bill Snyder looms behind her.

BILL

"Hey, Teena! Last day of school!"

TEENA

"Hi, Bill. Yeah, last day of school."

BILL

"So, I'm inviting you to my party this Saturday."

TEENA

"Oh. Bill, I don't like people who trap on my farm."

BILL

"What are you talking about?"

TEENA

"You know what I'm talking about. I shot at you."

BILL (avoiding her eyes)

"Well, whoever did it will probably get his traps out of there after that . . ."

TEENA

"If he can find his traps."

BILL

"What do you mean by that?"

TEENA

"No, Bill, I don't want to go to your party."

BILL

"We're going to sneak a keg in."

TEENA

"I don't drink beer."

Teena carries the two cokes to the table she is sharing with Chad.

CHAD

"So what did football boy say to you?"

TEENA

"He invited me to his school's out party."

CHAD

"And you said . . ."

TEENA

"I said no, you dummy. He's been setting traps at my place, and I shot at his pickup."

CHAD

"That guy can't seem to take a hint."

TEENA

"I don't see how it's a big deal that school's out; that just means more farm work."

CHAD

"It is a big deal, and I'll prove it to you."

TEENA

"O . . . kay . . ."

CHAD

"This Saturday evening when you're done with your chores, and, when Bill's having his party: drive over to my place. Bring Sweetie and Bugs with."

<u>TEENA</u>

"For what?"

<u>CHAD (smiles)</u>

"A picnic."

"Moody River theme" . . .

Teena, wearing blue jeans, a flannel shirt, a white cowboy hat and ponytail, drives her dad's pickup down a gravel road. Sweetie and Bugs are in the pickup bed, both leaning out to get the wind in their faces, Sweetie fox-grinning. Teena pulls into Chad's drive, where he waits, smiling.

<u>CHAD (opens the tailgate of her truck. Sweetie and Bugs jump down, the fox peering around in wonder).</u>

"Come on, you two. We're all going on an adventure.

Teena gets out of the pickup, gives Chad a kiss. They hug under the soft late-evening sky.

<u>TEENA</u>

"So—a picnic?"

<u>CHAD</u>

"It's not up to Bill's party, maybe. But you weren't going to that anyway . . . or did you change your mind?"

<u>TEENA (smiles)</u>

"You dumb cowboy. So where are we going to have our picnic?"

<u>CHAD (points to a rise beyond a valley of trees)</u>

"Up there, in the meadow."

<u>TEENA</u>

"We're going to walk all the way up there with picnic stuff?"

<u>CHAD</u>

"No, we're going to ride. Ta Da!"

He aims his arm at the barn, where two appaloosas are saddled, each bearing a picnic basket strapped behind the saddles.

TEENA (kisses him)

"You are one cool bookworm cowboy.

{Cut to} . . .

"Moody River theme":

Teena and Chad riding the horses down a dirt path into the valley of trees, shadows dappling the way, Sweetie and Bugs galloping behind, sniffing at the spring land.

They ride up the rise and come upon a grassy meadow. They unload the picnic baskets and Teena spreads a red-white checkered table cloth on the ground as Chad unloads the food.

TEENA

"No, Bugs, get away. Sweetie! Stay away from this food."

CHAD

"We've got cold fried chicken, deviled eggs, potato chips, apple slices and cold Cokes."

TEENA (helping to unload the food)

"Oh, this does look good. Did you make all of this yourself?"

CHAD

"Yes, I did."

TEENA

"You're lying. You made deviled eggs?"

CHAD

"Well, Mom made those."

TEENA

"And she fried the chicken too."

CHAD

"Well, technically . . . yeah. But I got the potato chips and the Cokes."

TEENA

"Bugs! Sweetie! Get away and stop nosing into our picnic."

CHAD

"Here, I'll get them away."

Chad draws a large hambone out of the picnic basket.

"Here, Bugs, this is for you. It's got plenty of ham left on it."

Bugs snatches the ham bone and turns away. Sweetie immediately grabs on to it and tries to steal it, until Bugs growls and shakes her away.

"Here, Sweetie, I've got one for you, a smaller one. But it's still got a lot of ham on it."

Sweetie snatches the ham bone and thumpers off to chew. Bugs finds his own place to chew. The meadow glows in sunlight as they munch their picnic dinner and talk about books. Prairie birds, meadowlarks, grackles, bluebirds, cardinals, orioles flicker in the trees around the meadow.

TEENA

"Your mom's a good cook."

CHAD (leans over to kiss her)

"She told me that if I let you slip away, I was an idiot."

TEENA (smiles)

"A good cook and a wise soul. Oh, this is good chicken."

CHAD

"And my potato chips are top of the line." (hesitates. They watch the sun slowly fall into the trees. Finally) . . .

"So, I suppose Bill's party's in full swing by now. How does this measure up to that?"

Teena looks at the appaloosas munching meadow grass. She looks at Bugs gnawing at his bone with a vengeance, at Sweetie gnawing at her bone. She looks at Chad gnawing a drumstick. She takes up a deviled egg.

TEENA

"No contest, bookworm. No contest at all."

{CUT TO} . . .

"Moody River theme"

Chad and Teena ride back down the valley trail, and up out of the trees and into a glorious sunset. Bugs lopes behind, the ham bone in his mouth. Sweetie gallops with her ham bone.

{FADE TO} . . .

Chad is changing the oil in his pickup. He takes off the oil pan nut and lets the old oil pour down into a pan. He hears a pickup pulling into the drive. He frowns.

Bill Snyder drives in and parks. He approaches Chad, who slides out from under the Ford F-150.

CHAD

"Bill; what's up?"

BILL

"I guess I need to talk to you."

CHAD

"About what?"

BILL

"About Teena."

CHAD

"What about her?"

141

BILL

"Look, I know you two are going together—and I won't get in your way. She wants you, not me. I won't try to change that."

CHAD

"Good."

BILL

"But . . . somebody stole some traps from me. Really expensive traps, and my old man's going ballistic over it. I need to get those traps back."

CHAD

"I don't know where your traps are."

BILL

"No . . . but it was Teena who got them. And I need them back."

CHAD

"Why would Teena have your traps?"

BILL

"I set them on her dad's farm, like an idiot. I shouldn't have set traps across the stream on their place. But Teena found them, and now she's got my traps, and they're worth a lot of money, and my old man's hot about it."

CHAD

"Hmmm. Well, I don't see how I can help you with this one. Believe me, Bill, I have no idea where your traps are."

BILL

Maybe you could ask Teena where they are. Ask her to give them back to me. I know she's the one who took them."

CHAD

"I'll talk to her about it. But nobody tells Teena what to do."

<u>BILL (looks away)</u>

"My old man's mad. I have to get those traps back. You know what they're worth?"

<u>CHAD</u>

"Not really. I don't know traps."

<u>BILL</u>

"But you know Teena. You know I'm sweet on her—but I know she wants you, so I'm willing to step aside. But I need those traps back, Chad."

<u>CHAD</u>

"The one thing I know about Teena is that she doesn't take orders. If you want your traps back—and if she's the one who took them—you're going to have to talk to her about it. Talking to me won't do any good."

<u>BILL</u>

"Will you try? I really need those traps back."

<u>CHAD</u>

"I'll try. And after that—good luck."

[FADE TO] . . .

Dad is sitting on the couch reading the paper, Sweetie curled up against him. Suddenly the phone on the end table rings, making the fox jump up in alarm and stare.

<u>DAD</u>

"Greene residence. Oh, Hi Charlie; what can I do for you?" (listens for a moment) "Somebody stole your traps? Hey, I know they're expensive. My land? Why would anybody trap on my land? You know I don't allow trapping. Oh, Bill is it. I know, I know; try raising a daughter. Well, I'm sorry, Charlie; I don't know where the traps are. I didn't take them, but if I'd have found them I'd have snapped them and thrown them into the creek. No, I didn't; I just told you I didn't take them. Yeah I know what they cost." (smiles at Sweetie who is staring at the telephone, her head cocked in curiosity) "Teena? I don't know but I'll ask her. Okay. Goodbye." (hangs up the phone, gives Sweetie a rub) "Never did like Charlie Snyder."

143

<u>TEENA (enters the living room, gives her dad a tentative look)</u>

"That was Bill's dad, wasn't it?"

<u>DAD (gives her a droll look)</u>

"Yeah. His dunce of a son was setting traps down by the creek. Somebody stole them."

<u>TEENA</u>

"I wonder who would do that."

<u>DAD</u>

"I don't know and I don't care. If I'd found them they'd be in the creek."

<u>TEENA</u>

"I think it was one of Bill's traps that killed Sweetie's mom."

<u>DAD</u>

"Probably. But I don't want to hear any more about it. I told Charlie that I didn't know who took the traps or where they are; leave it at that."

<u>TEENA (looks down at Sweetie who is giving her
the usual worshipful look)</u>

"I don't think he'll ever see those traps again."

[FADE TO] . . .

Time passes, and Sweetie grows into a beautiful young vixen. It is autumn. Dad sits in the living room with Teena. He is reading a farm magazine, she is on the floor brushing Sweetie.

<u>DAD</u>

"She's a full grown fox now."

<u>TEENA</u>

"I know. And you're such a pretty young lady. You are."

Sweetie Suddenly looks up as a noise echoes from outside: "Yip! Yip yip!"

Bugs looks up and growls. Sweetie stares at the dog door, her eyes wide.

TEENA

"It sounds like we've got a coyote out there."

Dad is watching Sweetie.

DAD

"You've got a full grown fox on your hands."

Again the noise: "Yip! Yip!" Sweetie runs to the dog door, and

Teena calls her back.

TEENA

"No, Sweetie, you stay inside. That coyote will eat you."

DAD (watching Sweetie, a sad look on his face)

"It doesn't sound like a coyote, Teena."

[FADE TO] . . .

That night Teena, Bugs and Sweetie are asleep in the bed. Suddenly Sweetie jumps awake at the sound from outside the dog door: "Yip!" She sits up in bed and stares. "Yip yip!" Sweetie licks Bugs on the face, nuzzling him. Bugs wakes up and groans sleepily. Sweetie jumps off the bed and pads out of the bedroom. Bugs watches her, then goes back to sleep. Sweetie disappears out the dog door.

[FADE TO] . . .

The next morning. Teena is out in the yard. Dad steps out on the porch and watches her.

DAD

"Chad just called. He's on his way over."

TEENA

"We're going to the library. Have you seen Sweetie? She wasn't in bed."

<u>DAD (a sudden sad look on his face)</u>

"I heard that thing yipping last night. Sounded like it was right on the porch."

<u>TEENA</u>

"Oh, God! What if Sweetie had to go potty and went out the dog door. What if a coyote got her?

<u>DAD</u>

"It wasn't a coyote." (looks down the road) "Here comes Chad."

<u>TEENA</u>

"I'm not going anywhere until I find her."

<u>DAD</u>

"I'll check the woods to the north; you guys check down at the creek."

[CUT TO]

Chad, Teena and Bugs wander, calling out Sweetie's name. Chad and Bugs search the woods south of the hill, while Teena wanders down in to the cedar grove.

<u>TEENA</u>

"Sweetie! Sweetie!"

Suddenly Sweetie appears out of the cedar trees and approaches Teena.

<u>TEENA</u>

"Oh, Sweetie, thank God! You bad fox, you scared me to death. Come on, bad fox, back to the house with you."

Sweetie hesitates, glances back at the cedar grove.

<u>TEENA</u>

"What's wrong, Honey? Where were you all night?"

Sweetie whines, glances at the cedar grove.

<u>TEENA</u>

"Oh . . ."

A male red fox peers out of the cedars. Sweetie stares at him, puts her head in Teena's breast and whimpers.

<u>TEENA</u>

"So that's it. A boyfriend."

[music—"Sweetie Theme"]

They hug, both crying. Teena remembers scenes of Sweetie as a baby, romping with Bugs, sleeping in bed, grinning as she munches her puppy chow, peering around Miss May's desk at the library, playing in the snow.

Sweetie cries and whimpers in Teena's arms, then glances back at the cedars where the male fox waits.

Teena takes the pink collar off Sweetie's neck. Sweetie sniffs it and cries.

<u>TEENA (wiping away tears)</u>

"It's time for you to go, Sweetie. You go where you have to go."

<u>SWEETIE</u>

"Yiii!"

<u>TEENA</u>

"I know. He's waiting for you." (hugs Sweetie, rubs her face) "You know, I was wrong; I was always wrong. You're not a bad fox; you're a good fox."

Sweetie cries, afraid, but keeps glancing back at the cedar grove.

<u>TEENA</u>

"Goodbye, my good fox. Goodbye, Sweetie."

Teena turns and marches away, sobbing her eyes out. Sweetie stares at her for a moment, then turns and scampers toward the cedar trees. The male fox appears, they touch noises; then Sweetie follows him into the cedars.

Holding the pink collar, Teena walks slowly up the hill toward the house. At the top of the hill Chad and Bugs meet her.

CHAD

"Teena, what's wrong? Did you find her?"

TEENA (bawling)

"I found her. But nothing's wrong."

CHAD (looks at the pink collar in Teena's hand)

"Why are you crying? Is she hurt?"

TEENA

"No, she's fine. I let her go."

CHAD (looks down at the cedar grove)

"Let's go bring her—"

TEENA

"No. Sweetie got a boyfriend."

CHAD

"A boyfriend . . . a red fox boyfriend."

TEENA

"Yes. She's going where she has to go."

Teena breaks out crying again, and Chad holds her, letting her cry on his chest.

CHAD

"Sweetie got a boyfriend."

TEENA

"She's going where she has to go."

CHAD

"What now?"

TEENA

"Now we go to the library."

As the music plays Teena and Chad walk slowly up to the house, Bugs following. Teena is leaning against Chad, crying. The pink collar dangles from her hand.

As the music swells, Bugs looks around at the cedar grove, his big face tragically sad, his eyes watering tears. Then Bugs turns and follows them up toward the house.

On the last chord of the music, the cedar grove blowing softly in the wind.

THE END.